LUMINA

Also by Seth Edgarde

LUMINA

A NOVEL BY

SETH EDGARDE

BLACKBIRD BOOKS

NEW YORK · LOS ANGELES

A Blackbird Original, April 2017

Manufactured in the United States of America.

The events and characters depicted
in this book are fictional.

Cataloging-in-Publication Data

Edgarde, Seth.
Lumina / Seth Edgarde.
p. cm.
1. DNA—Fiction. 2. Prions—Fiction. 3. Geomagnetic
field—Fiction. 4. Aurora borealis—Fiction. I. Title.
PS3605.D4564 L86 2017 813'.6—dc23 2016944069

Blackbird Books
www.bbirdbooks.com
email us at editor@bbirdbooks.com

ISBN 978-1-61053-038-5

First Edition

10 9 8 7 6 5 4 3 2 1

To Professor Greg, a bon vivant, who really did have more faith in me than I had in myself.

1

IT STARTED WITH THE BEES, dropping like snowflakes from the sky, dead, unable to find their hives and too exhausted to fly any further. It was only a small change, subtle, otherwise undetected, in the earth's magnetic field, but it threw their navigation system off. So they flew towards the sun, searching, until they died from exhaustion and fell, in a spiral, like Icarus and his lost wax, back to earth. They fell in clusters onto tennis courts in the Hamptons and fire escapes in the Bronx, in the water and on land, clogging power stations on the Lower East Side, shorting switches, and blocking drains. Jesse Wolfe was eating lunch with David Jenkins and paid no attention to the pitter patter on her roof.

She had never met him, but Jesse Wolfe had lunch with David Jenkins every day. She sat and watched him through the trading floor security cameras as they both ate. She had broken into the network the year before, when she was wreaking havoc on the Swiss banking system. They had almost caught her, but, in the end, she had gotten away clean, as always. She had even managed to transfer forty million euros from a Saudi sheik's numbered account to the National Council of Jewish Women at the last minute, just before she disappeared from the system. Even so, she took the chance and kept her link into the floor cameras at Deutsche Bank, so she could see David.

He was only a junior salesman, a minor player, but she was sure he would be very successful one day, and she was sure they would be together. So she sat in her painter's pants and t-shirt, legs folded on the chair, eating her tuna sandwich as she watched David eat his. In her semi-trance, she didn't notice the world unraveling around her.

The stories and images came over the grid of monitors that she had set up on the wall in front of her desk. No one noticed at first—just a small escalation in violence—but, as she stared at David, New York had reached its tipping point, and the pattern had become clear. People were attacking, even killing, one another: parents, children, even policemen. They were calling it an epidemic of insanity. But Jesse Wolfe was unaware, seeing only one man's face through the screen in her rundown flat on the top floor of her pre-war walkup and wondering what it would be like to kiss him.

A knock on the door snapped her out of her dream. She broke her gaze and looked at the other screens.

Chaos, havoc. And a beautiful stream of violin music that she could not identify. In the middle monitor, she saw the man on the other side of her door. The image of an arm jerking into another human being caught the corner of her eye from an adjacent monitor. The clock read 2:15. The knock repeated, louder. She stared at the door.

"Who's there?" she asked, feeling a tightening in her throat as she unfolded her legs and dropped her feet to the floor.

"Derek Remsen," the man replied through the door.

The dilapidated building on Avenue D was one of the few in Alphabet City that had not yet been gentrified. Although it was the "penthouse," the apartment had the musty smell of a basement. The walls had been scraped down, showing patches of bare plaster mixed with the faded pastel red of another century and forming a sort of odd Dalmatian pattern. The bare gray concrete floor was surprisingly solid, and the interior walls had all been removed years before, yielding an expanse of space, which, when coupled with the twelve-foot ceiling and carefully carved egg and dart molding, produced the majestic effect of decayed luxury.

There were only a few tenants who were still left, and, besides Jesse's clientele, a few drug dealers, and the odd grocery delivery boy from the local bodega, there wasn't much traffic in or out of the building. This, along with the spacious and oddly crumbling majesty of the building and the beautiful rooftop view of the East River, downtown and midtown Manhattan, and even the Con Ed switching station and Brooklyn beyond, made this Jesse's favorite place to work.

She opened the door.

He was only thirty, tall and unshaven, but the years had been unkind to him. There was a short but deep scar on his left cheekbone, which glistened off of his tan oilcloth skin. His long, greasy, blond hair was streaked with dark strands, all neatly combed straight back. His blue eyes were tight and cold and drew focus to his thin, slightly crooked nose.

He wore an off-white linen suit with a white button-down shirt and no tie, which, along with his three-day beard, presented a distinctly over-ripe version of the rugged image that men's casual wear catalogs strive to project. The dirty green saddle shoes with no socks and a splattering of unidentified dark fluid completed the picture.

His eyes rolled from her face, over her chest, and down her hips. He looked back up at her and smiled, wide and yellow. He licked his lips.

"I'm looking for Jesse. You his girlfriend?" he asked.

"I'm Jesse," she replied. "You're early."

"You're the fixer?" he asked, surprised.

"You got the money?" she shot back.

He reached under his jacket and into his back pocket and pulled out an envelope, thick with cash.

"Crazy shit going on out there," he said, as she finished counting the stack of hundreds.

"Yeah, crazy shit," she said, stuffing the money back into the envelope and sticking it into the back of her pants.

"Here's your new birth certificate, driver's license, and passport," she said, handing him a small packet. "Congratulations, you're now Derek Steinholtz."

He flipped through the items.

"Wow, these look totally real."

"They are real," she said, more insulted than annoyed.

He looked up at her, staring into her green Mediterranean eyes. He nodded.

"That's it?" he asked, with near disappointment.

"That's it," she said.

"What about—"

"It's all taken care of. The arrest warrants, your credit score, even your parking tickets."

The way his eyes shifted between her breasts, hips, and face unnerved her.

"You got a glass of water? It's hot out there."

She noticed a solitary drop of sweat roll down his temple and into the crevasse of his scar.

"Yeah, it's summer," she said, wanting him to leave.

"Crazy shit going on out there," he said.

"You already said that."

"Crazy shit going on . . . Crazy shit . . . Crazy . . . Crazy . . ."

In an instant, his pupils tightened, and his eyes locked in on hers. They were still blue, but they were no longer the same eyes. His face twitched, and he reached out to grab her. She stepped back, her heart pounding. The muscles in his neck tightened, and he pulled at his collar, suddenly gasping for air.

Jesse saw the blood drain from his face, and his eyes roll up into his head. He dropped to the ground, his body shaking like a suspension bridge in an earthquake. Jesse stood, frozen. Foam bubbled at the corners of his mouth. Within thirty seconds, he had stopped moving. The newly minted Derek Steinholtz was dead in the middle of Jesse Wolfe's doorway.

2

HE HAD SEEN BAD DAYS at the Ninth Precinct before but not like this. Amidst the noise of the squad room, James Samuel Delacourt, Jr. pored over the reports on his desk: A mother slitting her son's throat. A woman throwing her fiancé off a balcony. A police officer helping a rapist attack a woman. The last report, in particular, hit him hard.

Del had practically grown up in this station house. His father, Big Del, was a cop here for twenty-seven years. And he had been here for almost eight, himself, the last three as a detective. His father had always told him not to become a cop, but he could hear the pride in his voice the day he got his gold shield. Del Junior wasn't going to be just another beat cop, pounding the pavement, like his dad. He was a detective, with a suit and tie, and a desk.

But now, all bets were off. All hell was breaking loose, and Del knew that even the gold shields were going to have to go out onto the street to maintain order. He stared at the folder at the corner of his desk and the freshly-printed warrant next to it. The irony was hard to swallow. He had been looking for her for almost seven months. And now, it turns out, she was right down the street the whole time.

He opened the folder for yet another look. Jesse Wolfe smiled at him through the black and white photo with the grin of an arsonist. He ached to catch her. She had been on the NYPD's most wanted list for almost two years. She was also wanted by the FBI and the NSA. Meanwhile, the Pentagon had been trying to cut a deal to *hire* her.

She had taken down the IRS computer system for almost ten hours while distributing "Thanksgiving Bonus Checks" from the director's office to almost sixty-five hundred tax evaders. She made sure to include a personal letter of apology from the director "for being an asshole" with every check. She had medical grade marijuana delivered to troops overseas, every outstanding parking ticket in Levittown, Long Island voided, and a New York police captain's social security number reassigned to Michael P. "Mickey" Mouse. And yet, there was nothing on the computer about her at all. The only reason Del was able to find her was because she had started her career before things were fully computerized, so they still had some paper files on her. And she had left a connection open to one of the trading floors downtown. That had provided the key.

"Del!"

He looked up to see his captain's bald head leaning out his office door, gesturing him over. Spano was a small man but tough, in an old-school sort of way that reminded Del of his father. He had won two medals for valor, taking a bullet for his partner the second time, before making it to precinct chief. Del was glad he was in charge.

He closed the door behind him as he entered the office, still holding Jesse's folder in his hand.

"What are you working on?" the captain asked, his eyes landing on the folder.

It was a question Spano had asked him hundreds of times, maybe thousands, but there was something odd about it this time, something odd about a case status inquiry while the city was coming apart, street by street, minute by minute, and, although Del couldn't even articulate the thought, something odd about the way those eyes rolled down to the folder in his hand.

"I think I know where to find Jesse Wolfe," he said.

He knew that Spano would probably tell him to put the case on hold—the Ninth Precinct had bigger fish to fry at the moment—but he still girded to argue for her arrest.

"Go get her," Spano said.

Del pulled his head back, suddenly deflated by the man's lack of resistance and realizing the folly of it under the circumstances.

"Are you sure?"

"Yeah."

"But captain—"

"I said bring her in."

"You got it."

The rumble of the squad room, muffled through the glass office walls, spoke unintelligibly to the two men as they stood facing each other. Del had had dinner at Spano's house countless times, talking late into the night with the captain and his wife about every conceivable topic. He had sought Mrs. Spano's advice when his own marriage fell apart. He had mentored Spano's oldest son, when he was at the police academy. He had him deliver the eulogy at Big Del's funeral. He trusted the man with his life. But now, suddenly, he needed more.

The captain smiled and put his hand on Del's shoulder.

"No panicking. Not on my watch. For now, it's business as usual."

He then repeated the line that the men in his command had heard so many times before, "You know, public confidence is the first step in law enforcement."

Del exhaled a long breath and nodded. Yes, they had all been under the gun. Business as usual. Maybe that is the smartest thing. At any rate, at least he'd get to finally nab one Jesse R. Wolfe.

He thought of his ex-wife and their dead son as he walked down 8th Street, past the Budapest Café, where they used to meet for lunch. He could see Jesse's building at the corner, but his mind was still on his family. Teddy had been dead for more than three years, and Del hadn't seen or heard from Denise in almost two.

He had met her seven years earlier on the southbound IND platform at 59th Street, during afternoon rush hour on a hot summer day. A tall man with a Beatle cut grabbed her purse and made a run for it, knocking people over as he plowed through the crowd. Del, who had already been staring at her legs and ass, sprang into action. He caught the guy, and, holding him there in cuffs, got a date with the blonde in the white dress with the great legs. The crowd of hardened New York commuters broke into spontaneous applause for the first and only time in his career.

It turned out that she worked in the mayor's office in the PR department. She was from Council Bluffs, Iowa and had her degree in journalism from the state university there. Fresh-faced and trusting to a fault, she was, nonetheless, as shrewd and savvy as any Manhattan native. Even before their first date, she had managed to get a quarter page spread on Del and his heroics in the *New York Post*—"Cop Drops Mop Top at Subway Stop."

Even though it was almost a week's salary, Del took her to the Russian Tea Room on their first date. Within a year, they were married. It was only after Ted was born with a hereditary genetic disease that their relationship began to unravel. But even after their marriage crumbled, with two more miscarriages, and one set of divorce papers, they would still talk at least once every few days, and even meet occasionally for sex. Then her mother got sick, she went back to Iowa, and the phone calls stopped.

He put the image of her in all black, at Teddy's funeral, out of his mind as he walked up to the building on 8th Street and Avenue D, stepping over a strung-out junkie and crossing the threshold into the foyer. He looked at the names on the buzzers: Rodriquez 1B, Suarez 1C, D'Angelo 2A, Washington 3F, ... Then, finally, J. Lobo 7A—the penthouse. *Lobo*—wolf. It had to be her.

There was an odd thud echoing through the cavern-ous stairwell as he climbed flight after flight. When he reached the top floor, the huge steel door was open. It took Del an instant to realize that the man lying in the doorway was dead. He looked up across the threshold and locked onto a pair of green Mediterranean eyes. There was an instant of silence, and then Jesse turned and ran for the back window and the fire escape.

Del flew down the staircase to the sixth floor hall-way just in time to see her leap to the adjacent roof. He shot down the corridor, threw open the window, and followed. As he jumped onto the next roof, he could see her running a building ahead. By the time she had reached the end of the block, he had closed the gap by half.

She slid down the rusty ladder on the other side, pulling it free as she hit the ground. She had just enough time to bury herself in a dumpster. Just behind her, Del dropped the last twenty feet to the sidewalk, looked around. Nothing. He'd lost her. Then he heard the faintest sound amplified in the hollow metal cavity to his left. Movement. He turned to face the dumpster and kicked the side hard. A moment later, Jesse sprang out and bolted into the street, dodging traffic.

Del chased her down 9th Street as she bobbed and weaved through cars and people. Finally, he closed in on her at Tomkins Square, and, cornered against a hedge row and the men's lavatory, she stopped and turned to face him. She looked around in angry desperation and grabbed the nearest thing she could—boiling hot dog water from a pushcart—and threw it at him.

He ducked and came at her, as she scampered up a tree. When Del drew near, she kicked him in the chest, but he grabbed her leg, and they both went tumbling into the bushes. One move later, and he had her pinned face-down on the ground.

"Jesse Wolfe, you're under arrest."

As he lay on top of her, he could hear the envelope crinkle. He pulled it out of the back of her pants and waved it under her nose.

"Is this what they paid you to kill that guy?"

He knew this was bullshit even as he said it.

"I don't kill people. And stop touching my ass. Pervert."

3

DEL STOOD OUTSIDE the two-way mirror staring at Jesse, seated, alone at a table in the interrogation room. He went in and sat down across from her.

"What happened to the man in your doorway?" he asked.

She rolled her eyes. "Look, I told you I don't know. I did the guy a favor. He paid me. And then he had a seizure and died. And I guess you know the rest," she said, folding her arms in defiance.

"No, I don't," he said.

And he didn't. And by now, he knew that she didn't either. But *something* had killed him. The same something, he guessed, that was causing all the other havoc around the city.

"I did the guy a favor," she said. "A favor ... favor ... favor ..."

Jess's eyes rolled back into her head, and she began to shake. Drool slid out of her mouth, as she fell from her chair.

Del yelled at the two-way mirror. "Call 9-1-1!"

He bent down to perform CPR, pressing his lips against hers.

A minute later, two paramedics barreled through the door.

There was a man and a woman. The woman was small with narrow hips, a smoker's face, and a bad 1970s haircut. The man was younger and also slight, with bushy red eyebrows and thick red hair that, combined with his gunmetal eyes, gave him the look of an evil leprechaun.

There was dead silence in the room for what could not have been longer than one or two seconds but for what seemed like at least thirty. Del could feel his heart beat two, three, four times. There was no logical reason for him to know what was coming next, but his cop instincts told him.

The corner of his eye caught the glint of the EMT scalpel coming his way. He grabbed the latex hand of the woman, deflecting her stab and breaking her arm at the elbow.

Jess suddenly came to life, pulling herself up from the floor. Del stared in confusion. She stared back.

"Okay, I was faking it. So kill me," she said. Then her eyes widened.

With barely a second to react, Del saw those bushy eyebrows moving fast towards his prisoner. He grabbed the leprechaun's hand as it was about to thrust a screw-driver through Jess's chest.

He picked up the little man and hurled him through the two-way mirror. He stood, shocked, to see every cop in the precinct—all of the men and woman whom he had known for the past eight years including Captain Spano—standing on the other side, watching and wait-ing. He stared through a jagged rim of mirrored glass at people he had bowled with, gone to football games with, run the marathon with, people whose weddings and parents' funerals he had gone to.

They climbed in through the empty window frame and came for them. Jess stood, frozen. Del grabbed the long rectangular table from underneath and ran it through the broken two-way and into the crowd at chest level like a battering ram. He screamed with rage at what was happening. People went flying back into the observation room. The edge of the table struck the edge of the window frame at full force, catching a woman's left hand. Four of her fingers were severed and dropped to the floor like carrot sticks falling from a Ziploc bag. Del recognized the engagement ring. Miriam Wilson, the department secretary. She and her husband Jack had been married for fifty-five years. His heart felt like it would burst. But there was no time. He had to save his prisoner, as every good cop must do. And he had to save himself.

Del turned his head back to Jess, who was still standing, as if her feet were glued to the ground.

"Go! Get out of here! The back door!" He jerked his head toward the opposite wall. She turned, and, seeing the door behind her, lunged for the knob and opened it. Del dropped the table and made a dash for the back door, slipping through an instant after Jess. Two cops stood at opposite ends of the fluorescent-lit hallway. One ran towards Jess as the other drew his gun. Del shot the man dead.

"Let's get the fuck out of here!" she said.

She turned to run down the hall, but Del stopped her.

"It's a dead end. The only way out is back through the precinct room."

Del led the way, quickly dropping another bullet in the empty chamber. He couldn't bear to look at the body in blue as he slinked down the hall to a blind corner. As they approached, he motioned for Jess to hold up. He flashed a sliver of himself for no more than an instant, but it was enough to elicit a hail of small arms fire, including at least one automatic pump rifle. He estimated that there were three cops. He bared his head again, drawing more fire. Now they would need to reload. He grabbed Jess's hand and pulled her around the corner.

"We've got to get my keys. They're in my top desk drawer. I'll go around the side, draw fire; you grab the keys and head out the front door."

She looked at him, mouth half-open.

"Just do it," he told her. "It's a blue Crown Vic with a green front fender. Near the front gate."

There were fifteen or twenty cops scrambling around the large square room. The gun cabinet was open, and officers were reaching in and grabbing shot-guns, pistols, and other small arms. Even the desk sergeant stood, loading a double-action short barrel. Even in the war, Del had never seen anything like this. For a moment, he actually envied Jess: at least she was used to being hunted by the police.

Del touched Jess's arm, motioning her to his desk at the far corner of the room. As she moved, crouching low between the desks and chairs, Del jumped up and dumped over a large cabinet, expecting to draw fire. But they shot at Jess instead. She was the one they wanted dead. At least first.

As they converged on her, Del laid down cover fire. He landed a paperweight in a uniform's ear, dropping him to the ground, and shot the double-action from the desk sergeant's hands. He remembered being at the man's wedding three years before, shaking those same hands after the ceremony. He remembered wishing him a long life of happiness with his new bride. He thought of that bride's face, now, as he charged up to Jess, pick-ing her up from the floor and pulling her behind a pillar as he reloaded.

"Just stay behind me. We're almost there."

She nodded. Del was impressed by her composure. He had seen men in battle—good men, tough men—crack under fire. But Jesse Wolfe was holding her own.

Spotting a chair, he reached out, picked it up with one hand and threw it at the remaining cops. He then went low, holding Jess by his side, as he fired above the group's heads. In the momentary confusion, he popped open his desk drawer and grabbed the keys. They bolted out the door, just ahead of a shotgun blast.

His car was open, and they got in. Another shotgun blast shattered the driver's window before Del even had a chance to close the door. He pulled the car into reverse, tore back out of his space, and shot forward, slamming on the brakes to avoid hitting a cop with a single pump standing in their path. Jess looked over at Del, frozen, with his hands on the wheel. She could see the cop lift the shotgun at the windshield.

"Fuck!" she yelled, arching her left leg over the transmission hump and slamming her foot down on the accelerator.

The engine struggled against the brakes until Del let go. The car snapped forward, hitting the man with a pop and sending him through the air and into the back window of another car, even as he got off one last shot, blasting a hole though the windshield, exactly between Del and Jess.

They tore through the narrow side streets of Lower Manhattan, speeding to nowhere.

"Where the fuck are we going?" she asked.

"I don't know. Maybe Jersey."

"No. I have a place. It's on City Island. No one'll find us there."

"City Island?"

"Yeah. You know how to get there?"

There was the mild sarcasm of impatience in her voice.

"Yeah, I know how to get there, but you know, it *is* an island. If they do find us, we're trapped."

"It's on the water. I have a boat."

He looked at her. Who *is* this woman?

4

AS HE APPROACHED Grand Street from Ludlow, he felt a thud, low and hard on his rear quarter panel. He knew what it was even without looking—the blast from another double-pump. He looked in his rearview mirror and saw a squad car, this one from the 19th Precinct. There were two more behind that. Then, he saw another two, rounding a corner and closing in from Grand Street.

He darted through the intersection. The five cruisers filed in behind him.

"Where the fuck are you going?"

He reached under the seat and pulled up his own shotgun.

"You know how to use one of these?"

"Yeah," she said, in a tone less than reassuring.

"Good. The shells are in the glove box."

She held the gun in her hands as if it were a lunar rock. She opened the glove box and grabbed a handful of shells. She dropped them into her lap and picked one from the pile. A blast tore through the back corner of the roof, shattering the rear window and sending broken glass into her hair and down her back.

"Come on!" he yelled. "What are you waiting for?" It was then that he saw her holding the rifle, looking for a way to insert the shells.

"Jesus Christ!" He grabbed the gun and took it out of her hands.

"You drive! You do know how to do *that*, don't you?"

He moved to the side, as she slid over him. The shells rolled off her lap, onto the seat and into the foot well.

Gripping the gun with one hand, he reached down and grabbed the shells with the other. Then, in one effortless motion, he rolled each shell down into his fingers and pushed it into the slot in front of the trigger guard.

He could see her watching him out of the corner of her eye, as she sped up Ludlow. He rolled down the window and then thought better of it and simply aimed the gun through the hole in the rear. He squeezed the trigger and watched as the front tire blew out of the lead car, and it spun a 360.

Jess jerked the wheel to the right and punched the throttle to stop the car from fishtailing. The next car couldn't make the turn and flew out of control, causing the others to pile up like iron filings on a magnet.

Del turned and looked at her, surprised at her deft maneuvering. "Where did you get your license?"

Eyes straight ahead, she answered, "I don't have one."

As they made their way to the FDR, she noticed how quiet Grand Street was. Then she noticed the first body. He was just lying there in the road. Then there was another. And two more after that. Live people appeared before they got on the highway, but they seemed oblivious. Until they passed a man on the corner Essex, just in front of the Seward Houses.

He was old, probably in his seventies. She wasn't sure what she was looking at, at first. It looked like he was beating a rug. But then they saw it clearly as they sped by. He was beating another person. She looked over at Del with sad eyes, but he didn't look back.

"Just drive."

"Yes, sir."

She took them all the way to Pelham Bay Park before she spoke again.

"We need to ditch the car."

As they walked down Shore Road, Del looked out on the Sound. He could see King's Point on the other side, where he had gone to college at the U. S. Merchant Marine Academy. He thought of those happy days, as a young first lieutenant, before his two tours in Afghanistan.

It was hot out but humid—not like over there. And the green of the park's picnic area gave a feeling of normalcy that he never had during his service abroad. He knew it was an illusion, but he let himself enjoy the momentary peace as they continued across the Hutchinson River Bridge to City Island Road. They walked another three miles in virtual silence, past Orchard Beach and another picnic area, across City Bridge to the island.

It was a quiet, middle class community, less than half a square mile in Long Island Sound, looking more like a maritime village off the Maine coast than a disconnected piece of the Bronx. As they walked down City Island Avenue, Del watched the seagulls and smelled the salt air. He remembered boyhood trips to Orchard Beach with his father and cousins. All of a sudden, he felt very tired.

"It's down this street."

He followed Jess down a short side street which ended at the water's edge.

"This one."

It was the last house, right on the water. He could see a medium-sized motor boat bobbing at the dock. She unlocked and opened the front door. They entered and closed the door behind them. Jess let out a deep sigh. *Home sweet home.*

It was a Queen Anne Victorian, built some time in the later part of the nineteenth century, probably within a few years of Jess's East Village dive. But that was where the resemblance ended. Despite its age, the house showed no signs of deterioration. Every angle was straight and every wall, smooth, right up to the filigreed moldings where they met the characteristically high ceilings. Every door was thick, dark, rich oak. The front door probably weighed three hundred pounds. There was an ornate, rounded archway leading from the surprisingly large vestibule to the main hallway, supported by two fluted square columns of dark hardwood. Threadbare oriental rugs covered the hardwood floors, which were also still smooth and straight.

Jess entered the house as though she were coming home from a hard day's work, and Del, spying a collection of pictures on the hallway wall, adjacent to the staircase, had a suspicion. He walked in behind her, past the classic Victorian parlor with the stopped grandfather clock on the right, and the large, warm dining room, centered by a huge rectangular table with lion's feet on the left, to the wall of pictures.

He could see Jess's face through the child's look. There was a man in many of the pictures, with the same lips and teeth. There was one picture, much older than the rest, of a beautiful young woman. She had a different mouth but she looked out at Del with Jess's warm green eyes.

Jess was too tired to even acknowledge Del looking at her childhood. She was halfway up the steps by the time he turned to follow her. When they reached the second floor, she pointed to the left.

"You take that bedroom." Then, she pointed down the hall, the other way. "I'll sleep in there."

She took three steps down the hallway, anticipating the relief of tearing her clothes off, dropping onto the cool, squishy featherbed, and curling up around her favorite down pillow.

"Are you kidding? I'm not letting you out of my sight."

She stopped walking and turned back to face him, snapped out of her reverie and ready for a fight. "Listen, Buddy—"

He nodded his head with more protectiveness than authority. "I go where you go."

She was too tired to fight, and, besides, she knew he was right. There was also something about the way that he spoke those words that made her feel safe and cared for.

She nodded. "Fine. You sleep on the floor."

The room was almost as big as Del's entire apartment in Gramercy Park. It had dark maroon wallpaper with velvet flourishes. There were two long windows facing the front of the house and another large window and a smaller one facing the side. All of them, save the smaller window, which was an ornate, stained glass affair, had their shades drawn behind heavy maroon velvet drapes. The summer sun was just setting behind the red hues of the small, leaden window. There was a dresser, a full-length mirror, two large armoires, and two night tables on either side of the king-sized bed.

The room was hot and stuffy, and Jess felt a moment of resentment that she could not strip down to her panties and wrap her legs around the oversized pillow. She flopped straight back on the bed without even taking her shoes off. Del took the shells out of his pockets and put them on the floor. Then he pulled the shotgun out of his jacket and laid it down carefully next to the shells. He unzipped his jacket, took it off and then removed his gun harness and gun and put them on the nightstand.

He looked her in the eye. "I'm leaving the safety off. If anything happens, just remember: Aim for the center of the target, and squeeze the trigger hard."

She looked horrified as she pulled herself up, closer to his face, to meet his eye. "You mean if . . . if you turn into one of them?"

He didn't answer. She could hear the wooden floor creak under his knees as he got down on the rug beside the bed to sleep. She dropped back on the bed, eyes wide open, staring at the ceiling. *What was happening? Who was this man? Why weren't either of them affected? How many other people were still sane?*

She lifted herself up onto her elbows and then turned over in one swift motion to Del, who was lying on his side, facing away from the bed, with his jacket balled up under his head as a pillow. His long, deep breaths told her that he was already asleep.

"Um . . ."

She didn't even know his name. Then she remembered the other cops in the station house talking to him.

"Del?"

It was the first time that she ever called him by name.

He turned, eyes open, and faced her. "Yeah, what is it?"

She patted the bed. "Come up here on the bed."

He looked surprised. "Are you sure?"

"Yeah. You need some sleep. Just stay on *your* side," she answered, just a bit too defensively.

He got up, took off his shoes, and lay down next to her. She looked down, took off her own shoes, and laid back.

"Thanks."

"Yeah, no problem."

5

AFTER AN INITIAL two hours of peaceful slumber, Jess spent much of the rest of the night awake, staring at the ceiling. She could hear Del breathing, another human being nearby, which helped calm her, but her mind kept replaying the events of the day, over and over again. Derek Remsen dying in her doorway, the police staring through the broken two-way mirror before coming after her, the beautiful, unidentified violin music coming through her monitor.

She needed to make order of the chaos, and, for once, her brain simply couldn't. She wanted to hold Del's hand as she lay there, staring at imaginary patterns on the ceiling, but she didn't dare.

She drifted off, again, for an hour or so, just before dawn, but by six in the morning, the sun was seeping in through a crack in the drapes, and Jesse was awake for good. She looked over to see Del's eyes open and look over at her. She had wanted to savor the moment of consciousness, but his cop instincts seemed to be on full-time, even as he slept.

"I need a shower," she said.

"Don't close the door all the way," he replied.

She nodded, thinking to herself that she never did close the door all the way, not since she was three years old and found her mother dead on that same bathroom floor. At first, they had said it was leukemia, undetected and rapidly advancing, but, later, they had determined that it was a genetic blood disorder, a defect on the 19th chromosome, found primarily in Sephardic Jews. Her mother's family had been in New York for three hundred fifty years, but they still carried the same defective gene from the Iberian Peninsula. Her mother had never told her father, who, being a WASP blue-blood of Dutch-English descent, had given Jess a clean copy of the gene in question, thus ensuring that she would never get the disease. But, thanks to her mother, she would always be a carrier.

She had loved her mother, even as her memory faded, but she still held a rage deep inside, for not telling anyone about the disease, for having had the bad gene in the first place, for dying so young, and for making her a carrier. She knew that her mother had loved her but was too young when she died to ever remember her saying it. And there were so many times that she needed her mother to tell her, to say the words, *I love you.*

She thought of David as she stepped into the bath-room. How could she ever marry him—or anyone? Then she wondered where he was and what was happening to him, and sadness welled up inside of her, so that she was unable to enjoy finally pulling her clothes off and stepping into the warm shower.

Del had caught a sliver of Jess through the crack in the door as she undressed. He hadn't meant to and quickly looked away, but he was struck by her beauty. She emerged from the bathroom clean and dressed. Del afforded himself no such luxury, taking only a quick shirtless sponge bath at the ancient dual-spigot sink. He caught her staring as they spoke through the open door, and she blushed, losing her train of thought.

"I was saying that we should get online, check the TV and radio, make some phone calls."

"Yeah, of course."

He finished drying himself and put his shirt back on.

"You got a computer in this place?"

She rolled her eyes. "I'll see if I can dig one up."

She walked out of the room and waved him on. He followed her down the hall and through a door, into another room. This one looked like mission control at NASA. There was a huge flat screen monitor tucked neatly between two Victorian windows. The keyboard rested on a large, modern, steel and glass desk. There was another large control panel on the adjacent wall and a work table spread with electronics, a soldering iron, and two or three schematics. There was still an old four-posted canopied bed, yet another armoire, and a nightstand in the room. There was a raggedy brown teddy bear on the bed and a well-worn copy of *Anna Karenina* on the nightstand.

Jesse turned on the control center, and the monitor came to life. She sat down and began typing, as Del continued to take in the room, spotting three framed diplomas on the near wall.

"The Polytechnic University in the Borough of Brooklyn in the City of New York," he read out loud. "Jessica Renee Sweet."

He looked over at her, surprised.

"Jessica Renee Sweet?!" he said, at the same time incredulous and amused.

She looked up out of the corner or her eye, while continuing to type.

"Jesse Wolfe," she corrected him.

He had the urge to tell her what a pretty name she had and that she should use it more often, but he thought better of it. "Right. I guess they must've made a mistake."

"Yeah, must be," she replied, trying to mask her discomfort with sarcasm.

She'd obviously gone to great effort to expunge her birth name from the record but not before it made it onto her diplomas.

"Bachelor of Science in Physics, June, 2006, Bachelor of Science in Mathematics, June, 2007, Master of Science in Mathematics, June 2008," he continued. "Two bachelor's and a master's. Not bad."

"Yeah, whatever." She didn't take her eyes off of the monitor, which displayed a stream of cryptical commands and strings that were gibberish to his eye and made him feel a pinprick of inadequacy.

"So let's see, that would make you thirty-two."

It seemed impossible, but he *could* add.

She stopped typing and turned to him with feline eyes.

"I'm twenty-nine."

"Yeah, but—"

"I finished high school early, okay?"

"At fifteen?"

"Yeah."

"Oh come on, *fifteen*?" He knew she was telling the truth even as the words were coming out. His brain just couldn't catch up to his mouth in time.

"Hey, I won the fucking Westinghouse Prize. I was second in my class at Bronx Science. I would have been first, but that bitch in charge had it in for me."

She went back to her keyboard.

"So why aren't you a professor somewhere?"

She paused for an instant and sighed. "Because I had an asshole for an advisor."

"Let me guess, he had it in for you too."

"Something like that."

"You seem to piss a lot of people off."

"Yeah, maybe I do. So, what?" she said turning back to him. "Now why don't you tell me something: What's a guy who's smart enough to read the Latin off my diplomas doing working as a lousy cop?"

"Smart enough to read the Latin off your diplomas and smart enough to catch you," he added.

"You know *you're* really staring to piss *me* off."

"The feeling's mutual." He looked at her and shook his head. "I know your type. You think the rules are just there for you to break. I guess someone like you would have no idea about public service and working for the greater good."

"I worked for the CIA *and* the NSA for five years. I had at least a dozen papers published on cryptography. I helped them catch one of the biggest terrorists in the Middle East. I was their golden girl. So don't tell me about public service."

"What happened?"

"Look, just leave me alone. I need to concentrate, and like I said, you're really getting on my nerves right now." She continued to type. "It's your fault I'm in this mess to begin with."

"*My* fault! *You're* the one they want to kill."

He waited for an angry rebuttal, but she said nothing. In fact, she had even stopped typing. She sat, still as a lava-covered Pompeian fleeing Vesuvius, staring at the flat screen, expressionless. Del turned his head and looked at the flat screen too, and he stood, still and silent.

The screen flashed a composite of images: Union Square, Mid-Town, and Downtown. Then Uptown, the Outer Boroughs, New Jersey, and beyond. All of the scenes looked the same: Bodies. Everywhere. People gathering them up, hauling them off. And, throughout it all, other people going about their business as usual, as if everything were completely normal. There was an occasional thrust of violence or scream or cry. But it was quick, leaving the feeling of illusion, as if it had never happened. And, strains of music, classical, unidentifiable, weaving in and out of the background.

Jess typed a few keystrokes, and up went scenes from Harrisburg, Pennsylvania. More of the same. Then Winnipeg, Montpellier, Macau, Kyoto, Jakarta. All the same.

It had not occurred to either one of them before then that what was happening might be more widespread than the lower half of Manhattan.

Jess pulled up the screen at Deutsche Bank to look for David, but the trading floor was empty. Staring at the deserted desks, Del thrust his hand into his pocket with the force of panic and pulled out his phone to call Denise, suddenly needing to hear her voice. The phone began to ring. But anticipation turned to dread as it continued to ring with no answer.

They turned on the TV and then the radio. They looked at more scenes from the hidden camera network that Jess had hacked into. Some radio stations played nothing but music, usually classical. Others broadcast news only, as if nothing were wrong. A few stations were dead—or so it seemed—with occasional patterned blips in the static. And one station was actually giving reports on what was happening. There was a similar pattern for the television.

Del tuned Jess's stereo to 1010 WINS. They were reporting an epidemic of insanity. It was worst in urban areas, particularly Manhattan. Other reports on the television simply said to stay home and lock your doors, hastening to add, unconvincingly, that there was no reason to panic. A few areas, including the eastern end of Long Island, didn't seem to be affected, yet.

They turned to the internet. Various blogs, podcasts, and other postings contained a mix of hysteria, vitriol, delusion, and calm resignation. Some people were declaring the end of the world. Others saw nothing amiss. Del joked, uneasily, that at least on the blogosphere it was business as usual. He was trying to comfort Jess. He could see in her eyes and uncharacteristic serenity that her imagination was running wild.

"I have to go find my boyfriend," she said, looking at Del and starting to get up.

He gently pushed her back down in the seat. "You're not going anywhere. It's too dangerous. And you're still my prisoner." He paused for a moment, detecting a level of vulnerability in her tight shoulders.

"I'm sure he's fine."

She looked up at him.

"*Are* you?"

She had a way of cutting through the layers of words and phrases that was both breathtaking and unnerving at the same time. He opened his mouth to try again but stopped. The flat screen had caught the corner of his eye. He could see the grounds surrounding the house that they were in. There were at least two dozen armed men closing in. He turned and stared at the screen.

"We've got to get out of here!"

She looked back at the screen and got up. This time, he didn't stop her.

"The boat," she said.

Dread shot through Del's gut. The memory of a spring day, just across the Sound, off of King's Point, wrapped itself around his being and squeezed.

"We'll shoot our way out," he replied.

"Are you fucking nuts? I don't even know if we can get to the *boat*."

He nodded, reluctantly. Then a Molotov cocktail flew through the window. The fire spread quickly, as they ran out of the room and down the hall.

"There's an elevator!" cried Jess.

A cacophony of automatic gunfire sent an avalanche of glass and wood in all directions. When they reached the elevator at the other end of the hall, Jess threw the door open, and they tumbled in. Another Molotov came through the now empty window frame and landed at the foot of the elevator just as Del slammed the door shut. Jess pounded the black plastic button marked "B." She turned to Del. They were knotted together like a ball of rubber bands.

"The basement. There's a tunnel leading out to the pier."

The drum beat of bullets lowered with them to the first floor. The polished brass of the ancient Otis elevator pinged and bent but did not break under the assault.

Then came the flamethrower. Gasoline and flames spread over the first floor and consumed the house which had stood for one hundred twenty-five years at breakneck speed. Halfway between flame-engulfed floors, Del pulled the lever and stopped the slow but steady motion of the coffin on pulleys.

He stood and punched his fist through the trapdoor in the roof.

"Brace yourself."

Jess stood, as Del raised his shotgun, took aim and shot the cable in half. The elevator plummeted through the flames and crashed in a ball of dust into the basement floor.

"You okay?" he asked, as he disentangled himself from her and struggled to stand.

"Fine."

She was slower to get up, and he could tell that her knee was hurt. His own ankles were aching, as he pulled the door open and helped Jesse out. She broke hard left to a double metal door. There was a padlock. Del shot it apart with his .38, and Jess pulled the doors open. They darted through the tunnel to a short steel ladder. Jess grabbed the key to the boat from a small hook and clambered up to a manhole-cover-like trapdoor at the other end. Del came up behind her, popped the lid, put his hands on her ass, and pushed her into the light at the foot of the pier. Then he pulled himself up as she waited for what seemed like seemed like at least a minute but was no more than five or six seconds.

They had caught their attackers completely by surprise. They were half way down the pier, before any of them even noticed that the house was empty. When they spotted them approaching the speed boat, they opened fire. Jess got in first. Del stood at the water's edge.

"You go ahead. I'll hold them off," he said, with fear masquerading as chivalry.

"Are you fucking crazy? I can't do this alone. Get your ass in here!"

He looked back. There were five of them approaching the pier and running fast. Several more were heading for the boat.

She took his hand, sensing his not-so-well-disguised panic. "Come on. It'll be okay."

A bullet whizzed between them. He looked back at the men running down the pier, held his breath, and jumped onto the boat. She started the engine as he unmoored it with the deft moves of an old sea hand. They sped south, past Big Tom and Belden Point, into the open Sound.

6

Shelter Island, at the far tip of Long Island, would have been a logical choice even if Del didn't have a summer timeshare there. At nearly a hundred miles from the city, it was isolated enough to be unaffected by the maelstrom, yet still close enough to civilization to have the TV, radio, and internet services that they would need to figure out what was going on and decide what to do. It was also easily accessible by boat.

As Del set the course, he stared out the port side at King's Point and the Merchant Marine Academy. His mind wandered to that spring day, almost ten years earlier, when he had almost drowned off the Stepping Stones Lighthouse. He could just see it out of the corner of his eye, as he turned away. Then he snapped out of it and realized.

"Hey, we're going the wrong way," he yelled.

Jess didn't seem to hear him, so he got up and went over to her in the pilot's chair, leaned in, and pointed to the Empire State Building ahead of them in the distance.

"Shelter Island is *east* of here, *away* from the city."

She continued to stare straight ahead. "I grew up in that house. Every picture of my father was in there. And my mother. My great-grandfather built that house. Those fuckers aren't getting away with this."

"Look, I'm sorry, but we are *not* going back to the city. It's suicide. Now turn this boat around."

She ignored him, and they continued to zoom along the water, the skyscrapers of Manhattan getting closer by the instant, until he could no longer afford to negotiate. He grabbed her from behind, wrapping his massive arms around her, picking her up, and moving her out of the pilot's bay.

"Let me down! You fucking asshole!"

He held her with one arm and turned the boat around with the other, even as her protests grew more violent.

"You goddamn fucking asshole! This is my boat. It's my goddamn boat! Get the fuck off my goddamn boat!"

As they passed City Island, the light from the flames consuming Jess's girlhood home flashed off her eyes, and she finally stopped struggling.

"I'm sorry, Jessica. I really am."

It was the first time he had called her by name, and he didn't even realize his error. Normally, she would have been furious, but, at that moment, it actually made her feel better. It was the name her parents always called her. And it *was*, after all, her real name.

Her breathing slowed, and her thoughts drifted back to David. It was now about 3:30 in the afternoon, and she couldn't get him out of her mind, until finally, she fell asleep. It was dusk when she awoke. Del was still at the wheel, pulling the boat to the dock on Shelter Island. She watched him steer with the mastery of an experienced pilot, and it made her wonder why he seemed so afraid of the water back at City Island.

She had an eerie feeling as she stepped off the boat and took in the town. The atmosphere was one of a quiet, seaside tourist town on a lazy summer's eve, except there were no people. There were boats for rent for both harbor tours and fishing; there was a bait shop, several souvenir stores, and a place to rent bicycles. There were seafood restaurants and corndog stands. But everything was closed.

It was bigger, nicer, and cleaner than City Island, but it gave Jess the creeps. Even the beautiful multi-colored sunset was no help, though she did notice it. For a moment, she even thought she saw the flash of the Aurora Borealis, the Northern Lights, but at just of 40 degrees north, it didn't seem possible, especially not in the summer.

"Is it usually like this?" she asked Del.

"No," he answered, sliding the safety off his pistol.

They walked almost two miles inland to Del's time-share. It was like a ghost town the whole way, until they reached the house. It was a Craftsman bungalow, framed by two cypress trees and a slightly overgrown hedge. Low to the ground with neat horizontal lines, the house was smaller than it looked but appealing.

There was a light on inside, and, as they approached, a noise. Talking. People. Del drew his service revolver and gestured, in the military style of a point man in combat, for Jess to stay back. She followed him anyway. He tapped on the door with the gun, laying back, outside of the frame. There was no answer, so Del pounded the door hard with his fist.

"Come on, it's Delacourt, open up!"

He could just hear the sound of a foot stepping on dirt behind him, when Jess yelled his name. He spun around, his finger hair-trigger, ready to fire the pistol now pointed at another man's face. That man had his gun pointed right back at him.

They stared at each other for a long moment. Del knew the man. It was his former partner, Eric Colton.

"Shoot him!" Jess yelled. "What the fuck are you waiting for?!"

But Del's cop mind told him not to. If Eric had been one of *them*, he would have already shot both him and Jess from behind, when he had the chance.

"What are you fucking doing? Are you crazy?" she screamed.

"Shut up!" he yelled back at her, as he re-holstered his gun.

But Eric was still pointing his. He cocked the trigger, his eyes hard with pain and fear.

"It's okay, Eric," he told him. *"We're okay. We're okay too."*

Eric sighed out, uncocked the gun, and lowered it to his side. Del stepped over, put his arm around him, and looked at Jess.

"Jesse Wolfe, Eric Colton. My partner at the 9th."

Jesse Wolfe never liked authority, and cops were the worst. The very idea of such people—specially appointed, who could tell her what to do and how to do it—irritated her to no end. In a way, a precinct full them shooting at her was just the natural progression in her relationship with the law and authority in general.

There was a time when she tried to fit in, when she went to work for the CIA after she finished her master's degree. Things started off on the wrong foot right away, when they made her dress up for work—a skirt and pantyhose—every day, even though she was doing cryptanalysis in a back office cubicle and never dealt with the public. Through her sheer brilliance, she was actually rising up through the ranks, despite constantly butting heads with her boss, an old school political animal who didn't appreciate subordinates, especially pretty young women, who were smarter that he was.

Things came to a boil one day when he ignored her warnings of an impending market square bombing in Herat, Afghanistan. Almost forty people were killed, including women and children. It was the final straw.

Jess barged in to a meeting, threw the report down on the conference table, and called her boss a fucking idiot in front of two generals, the director of the NSA, and an aide to the president. She quit on the spot then took off her heels and pantyhose right in front of everyone and threw them at him.

"Here, you wear these!" she yelled, before storming out, barefoot.

An hour later, the cops showed up at her apartment and arrested her for assault and battery. It was bullshit, and everyone knew it. But they still charged her, taking her fingerprints and subjecting her to a strip search. She was out on bail a couple of hours later and eventually got the charges dismissed, but she hated cops more than ever.

And now, here she was, in a cop timeshare.

"Do you really think it's smart coming here after your entire precinct tried to kill me yesterday?" she asked Del.

Eric looked at his former partner, surprised. She had a point.

"It was a calculated risk," he said.

"Do us both a favor and leave the calculating to me," she snapped back.

"You got a better idea?" he asked.

Eric shook his head. "Jesus Christ. You two are like a married couple. Knock it off. You're here now."

"Yeah, sure, whatever," she said. "Is there anything to eat around here?"

7

JESS FLIPPED THROUGH the channels of the TV as they ate soda cracker tuna sandwiches and drank water. The situation had deteriorated markedly, even from that morning. Ninety percent of the stations were now static. About half of those left were broadcasting nothing but crop and weather reports. The remaining handful streamed numbers across the screen at breakneck speed.

They figured that the radio would be more of the same, but they were wrong. About half the stations were sending out streams of computer tones similar in sound to a fax machine, or, Jess thought, and old acoustic modem. Other stations still broadcast nothing but classical music, but much of it was now unfamiliar.

It was only on the thirty-one meter band of their shortwave radio that they were able to get any real news at all, and even then, only in bits and pieces on different frequencies, although the reception was particularly good, especially for the summer.

"There's been a lot of sunspot activity this year and a couple of huge solar storms. Does weird shit with the radio reception," she explained to the two cops.

The internet proved more fruitful. There were blogs and chat rooms, pictures and video clips.

The country was under martial law, with even rural areas now affected. In fact, the rest of the world was also in turmoil. They watched clips of the madness that they had already seen on the streets of New York replayed in the alleyways of London, the boulevards of Paris, farms in North Dakota, cities in China, the plains of Africa, and the jungles of South America.

No one seemed to know exactly what was causing it—some theorized that it was a particularly virulent virus—but the effects were clear: People were going insane. Many of them became violent and many became sort of automaton savants, with incredible abilities in music, math, and languages. Some were traveling together in gangs, savages hunting other humans as their prey. Others seemed to descend into a sort of obsessive-compulsive purgatory, writing numbers or equations until they dropped dead of exhaustion.

Jesse probed further, tapping into traffic and office camera networks and then the NSA satellite network. The scenes were devastating and getting worse and more widespread. There was random violence from ordinary citizens with no provocation. Chaos was subsuming order. Then, in a shocking contrast, they would see other places abandoned or virtually so.

"Check the Center for Disease Control in Atlanta," said Del.

She nodded. *Probably not a bad idea.*

The CDC indicated that it might be a virus, but, in any case, it seemed to be some kind of infectious agent, and it was growing exponentially—that is, with the power of an exponent, geometrically, doubling and doubling and doubling until the entire planet would be overrun. It would be the end of the world, the end of humanity.

Suddenly, everything else receded into the background.

"How is it spread?" Del asked.

"Food, water, who knows?" Jess replied.

They all looked at each other and at their dirty plates and cups.

"Why aren't we infected?" he asked.

"Maybe we are," Eric chimed in.

Jess shook her head. "It would've gotten us by now."

They paused to consider this for a moment, but nobody said anything more. Jess typed in a numerical IP address into her web browser and up popped a polished but flamboyant-looking screen. Jess logged in under the name Jess C. James.

"What's this?" asked Del.

"An underground chat room."

"For criminals?"

She sighed. "Stop being a cop for five fucking minutes, would you?"

A popup appeared on the screen stating that she had a message from "Dr. Love." She turned slightly red and clicked on the link. The messaged read: *Hope you are ok. Been looking for you. Very worrisome stuff. Maybe you have some thoughts. I know I do.*

He left a link, which Jess clicked.

"Who the hell is Dr. Love?" Del asked with a tone approaching jealousy.

"He was my advisor in grad school."

"I thought you said he was an asshole."

"Come on," she said impatiently to the screen, which was still loading, the issue of her advisor clearly embarrassing her. "We worked together on the Human Genome Project."

"Aren't you a mathematician?"

"Yeah, it's computational biology, bioinformatics," she said, turning to him. "Gene finding."

They both stared at her.

"Basically, I used the mathematical methods of cryptography to help him decode human DNA. The same way you'd crack a password by decrypting it, you could view DNA as a giant cipher and then crack it by the same mathematical methods that you use to crack computer passwords."

"You guys must have hit it off great."

The link brought them, at last, to the doctor's blog. Jess looked at his face with familiarity, as the video clip played on the screen:

I believe that the difficulties that we are currently experiencing are not, in fact, due to a virus, as some have speculated. The erratic, violent, and pathological behavior, the personality changes, the deterioration in personal habits on such a widespread scale can, in my opinion, be caused by only one type of infectious agent: prions.

For those of you unfamiliar with the term, a prion, or a proteinaceous infectious particle, is not actually a life form or even alive in any sense of the word. It is simply a rogue protein, structurally deformed in such a way as to cause the tissues of the brain to unravel, the way a run in a stocking causes the threads of the fabric to unravel. The resulting physical changes to the individual's brain, in turn, change who and what they are and what they might be capable of.

Prion diseases have been around for as long as there have been people on Earth. Mad Cow Disease is the best known example, but there are others. There is no known treatment or cure. It is not clear exactly how the disease spreads, or if some people might be immune.

Since they are not actually alive, prions are exceedingly difficult to destroy. They are impervious to heat, cold, and radiation.

An instant later, the video froze. Jess eyed the modem then popped up a window showing their network traffic.

"What's happening?" asked Eric.

Jess shook her head. "We lost our internet connection."

She slumped back in her chair.

"Can you get it back?"

She shrugged. "I'll try again later."

Del got up. "I'm going to grab a quick shower," he announced.

Eric nodded, reassuringly, but an uneasy feeling welled up under Jess's ribcage.

"I'm going with you," she said, blushing an instant after the words were out of her mouth.

"I usually shower alone," he grinned, pausing while she squirmed in embarrassment. "Don't worry, I trust Eric with my life."

"Okay," she said.

He smiled at her for the first time, and it sent a rush through her, causing her to look away. He turned and headed down the hall, disappearing up the stairs, grinning even wider.

Jess continued to poke and probe at the down connection, but she knew it wasn't coming back.

"My brother-in-law is a mathematician," Eric said.

"Huh?"

"My brother-in-law. He's a mathematician. He works for one of the insurance companies."

Jess hated small talk. And she particularly hated it when people tried to find something in common with her. And, even though Eric seemed like a nice guy, she still hated cops.

"Look, no offense, but I don't feel like talking much right now."

He pulled his hands back in annoyance. "Suit yourself."

A minute later, when she had completely given up on the computer, she turned to him, suddenly curious. "What kind of partner was he?"

"I thought you didn't want to talk," he said sarcastically.

"I'm sorry about that."

He nodded. "He's the best of them. Took a bullet for me once."

She thought how there was no one alive who would do the same for her, and it made her sad. A heavy thud, like a body slamming against a wall, broke her thought. She looked at Eric. *The bedroom. Del.* They bolted out of their chairs and down the hall, sucking up the short staircase, Jess a step behind Eric.

Del had seen that the TV was on the second he had entered the bedroom. It hadn't occurred to him that anyone else was in there, because there was nothing but static coming out of the screen through the darkness. When he saw it flicker off Spano's face as he sat, half-grinning in the corner, his heart sank.

He looked at Del with a slow turn of the head, his expression fading. "You know you're like a son to me, but orders are orders."

Del noticed the .38 in his hand as he heard the door shut behind him. He turned to see another man, naked, scribbling numbers on the wall. He knew he didn't have the heart to shoot Spano, even if he were quick enough to get his gun out in time. But his emotions veered away from sadness to frustration and rage, and his body took over.

He grabbed the man behind him, lifted him like a ragdoll, and threw him across the room at Spano. The man's body smacked hard against the wall, arms flailing, while the captain ducked out of the way. Then Del threw the nightstand, knocking the gun from the Spano's hand. He reached for his own gun, while the naked man got up and charged him. Del shot the man dead.

The door popped open. Eric stood for a second, absorbing the scene. But Spano didn't waste a second. The gun back in his hand, he fired two shots, dropping Eric to the floor, even as Del ran at him and took the gun away. He punched his captain only once, but it was enough to knock him out cold. Then he sat on the floor, sweating and breathing hard. When he got up, Jess was cradling Eric in her lap. His eyes were rolled up in his head, and he took two last breaths. Jess looked up at Del and shook her head.

Del pressed the butts of his hands into his temples, squeezed his eyes shut, and paced back and forth exactly once, as if completing some ritual that closed down a certain part of his brain. He grabbed Jess's hand.

"Come on, let's get out of here."

She stood but, like Lot's wife, looked back as she exited the room. She stopped dead in her tracks. The near wall was covered with numbers. Del looked back, finally noticing.

"What does it mean?" he asked.

"I . . . I . . . I think this is a sequence from e."

"What?"

"Euler's number. You know, little e, the base of the natural logarithms. It's the base number that they use to model exponential growth."

8

DEL CARRIED HIS PARTNER'S body back across the island toward the boat. His arms ached under the weight. Jess knew he was in a fragile state and didn't want to do anything to make it worse. She had let him leave Spano sprawled unconscious on the bedroom floor, even though she knew better than to leave him alive. *There are so many of them now, what difference would one more make?* She rationalized.

But, somehow, Spano had known where to come to find them. It *was* Del's timeshare, but still, it seemed like he *knew* Del would be there. She wondered if he had been there at City Island too. It had been gnawing at her ever since they left the house, and now it finally dawned on her. *They traced the internet connection*. It sent a chill down her back.

When they found their way to the dockside, Del lowered his friend's body onto the boat.

"What are we going to do with . . . him?" Jess asked gingerly.

"Eric. His name is Eric. We'll bury him at sea," Del told her, stepping on the boat. "I don't suppose you have a flag?"

"Yeah, actually I do."

"Good," he said, pausing for a moment. "Thanks, Jesse."

She liked it when he called her by name but had an odd pang for him to call her Jessica again. Then she remembered the house burning down earlier in the day and felt her own stab of pain. It seemed like a lifetime ago. She unmoored the boat and got on board.

The Aurora Borealis was in full bloom now, lighting up the sky with its rainbow of flashes. It was so odd and rare this far south, and in the summer, but she had too much else to think about now, too much to do.

"Let's get out of here," she said. "By the way, where the hell are we going?"

"Let's move out into the Sound. Lie low, get some sleep, figure out what to do next."

They slipped out of Dering Harbor, out into Gardiner's Bay, then around Orient Point, and into the open Sound, leaving Shelter Island and Del's cop timeshare behind.

When they finally dropped anchor along the state line, at the fattest part of the Sound, halfway between Riverhead, New York and Short Beach, Connecticut, it was almost 3 a.m. They weighted Eric's body down with sandbags and slipped him out from under the flag into Long Island Sound. Del didn't say a word. He was too choked up to even try. Jess had the urge to hold his head to her breast and stroke it, but she didn't dare.

They watched the small foam swirl dance around the surface after the body disappeared. Unable to contain herself any longer, Jess finally reached out and squeezed Del's shoulder. He reached back and squeezed her hand. Then they broke contact. It was awkward, but it was something, something *human*, soothing to make each of them want to continue, to find others, to live.

They took turns sleeping until past midday, when they were both up for good. Jess knew they were going to have to find Dr. Love, a.k.a. Professor Daniel David Lovejoy, PhD, her former advisor, even though she hated the idea.

"Do you have any idea where he might be?" Del asked.

"He teaches at Stony Brook. I followed him there when I went for my PhD. But he's also got his own lab at Brookhaven."

"How do we know which one he's at?"

"I'm guessing he's at Brookhaven. That's where he shot the video clip we saw yesterday. Besides, he spends most of his time there."

Jesse Wolfe had spent a lot of time in that lab herself. It was an amazing place for a young graduate student in Applied Mathematics. She hadn't initially been interested in computational biology, preferring the more traditional areas of mathematical cryptology, but the math *was* basically the same, and she grew to love the field. She even had it in her mind that one day she would figure out what exactly her mother had died from, what *she* carried in her own genes.

It never happened. Her relationship with Lovejoy fell apart. He kept the lab; she went to the CIA.

She pulled out a map of Long Island, planting her finger on the centerline of the land mass, about two thirds of the way to the end.

"It's in Upton."

Del looked at it on the map: *Brookhaven National Laboratory*. He noticed that it was adjoining a *Naval Weapons Center* on the same compound.

"I think we should have a look before going in. If we pull up to shore, maybe around Wildwood, we can get in close enough, probably within about five or six miles of it. You have a pair of binoculars?"

She rolled her eyes. "Yeah, I have a pair of binoculars," she said, her tone making him feel stupid, like he was missing the whole point.

"What's the problem then?"

"If *they* spot *us*, we're screwed."

"Yeah, but if we get there, and they're in lockdown, we'll be screwed even worse."

She thought for a second and nodded. He was right. "Security *is* usually kind of tight there."

Del piloted the boat in, slowly, quietly, until they were only a few hundred yards offshore. He cut the motor. Jess produced a pair of ancient binoculars.

"Are those Navy surplus?"

"No, they were my grandfather's," she answered, putting them up to her eyes.

"Was he a sailor?"

"Shipbuilder."

Del nodded in approval, even though Jess was still focused on the landscape of Long Island.

Finally she spotted it. Brookhaven. But it was no longer the friendly research lab that she remembered. Uniforms were everywhere. The place *was* in lockdown. It appeared to have reverted back to being a full-blown military base, as it has been in the 1940s. Soldiers were definitely running the show, and they appeared healthy, but it was hard to tell for sure.

She and Del took turns with the binoculars. There *were* some bodies. Soldiers carried them to what appeared to be a makeshift crematorium at the edge of the compound. There was also some construction going on. Jess spotted three new transmission towers and a building that looked like a new lab, and Del identified at least three new barracks and a huge ammo dump.

"It looks like they're getting ready for World War III," she said.

"Looks like standard military protocol to me."

They watched for no more than twenty minutes but it seemed like hours. Then a woman climbed out a window and broke into a run. Two soldiers pounced, dragging her off, while she bit and scratched at them. Another man came up to the front gate in civilian clothes and appeared to have some kind of fit. Another soldier went down on one knee and dropped him with a single shot.

"Is *that* standard protocol?" Jess asked, handing him the binoculars.

He looked and then said ruefully, "Under the circumstances, it could be."

"Yeah, and maybe not," she said. "I mean, how the hell do we tell which are the infected ones?"

"I don't know," he said, pausing for a moment. "But I have an idea."

He put the binoculars down.

"If we go in like military personnel, in uniforms, proper military vehicle and all that, we'll be covered," he told her. "If the soldiers running the place are infected, they'll figure we're with them. If they're not, it'll at least make it easier to get in and see Lovejoy. Either way, we'll look like we belong."

It made a certain amount of sense, but it was very risky. Then again, Lovejoy seemed like their only chance.

"Okay," she said. "But where are we going to get uniforms?"

9

DEL HADN'T BEEN BACK to King's Point in ten years, since the day he almost drowned, but he was glad he'd get to see the place again. College was a happy time for him, and, if he was to meet his end, he preferred to do it in the dress blues of the Merchant Marine. They were about fifty miles east of the academy but decided to wait, hanging back in the Sound until dark. Del was a man at peace with himself as he sat, playing cards on deck with Jess. She, on the other hand, seemed vulnerable out on the open water, and a creeping feeling of dread began to take over as night fell.

"Gin!" Del exclaimed, laying his cards on the table, but Jess hardly even looked.

Then, something seemed to catch her attention. A noise. Del heard it too, behind him. A motorboat, white and orange, off in the distance, getting closer, speeding right at them. He could see the man at the helm: Spano.

"Anchor up!" he yelled, moving to the stern.

But it was too late. It had closed within a hundred yards. He grabbed Jess and pushed her head down onto a life preserver before lowering his own to brace for the impact. Waiting, it seemed like an eternity, and, for a second, he imagined it wouldn't come. But he knew better, and a moment later, the thud threw them across the deck.

The Turing jerked hard to the starboard side, and he thought she might go over, capsize, but she slid back on an even keel, having taken the blow. He got up and saw his old captain crumpled, bleeding on the far side of the deck, having been thrown clear, across the gap between the two boats. Not sure if he was dead or alive, Del hesitated. But the man's eyes opened.

He looked at Jess then up at a pole hook on the side rail, just above him. Grabbing it, he got to his feet and came at her. Del grabbed the other end, avoiding the sharp hook, and pulled. But the man wouldn't release it, and they struggled. Finally, Del pushed it sideways, and Spano lost his balance and went overboard.

Del went to the side, looked into the water, and saw his friend, boss, and mentor disappear under the surface. He wanted to go in after the man, but Jess stopped him.

"He's gone," she told him. "I'm really sorry."

He nodded, silent, then pulled up anchor, stepped into the pilot's bay, and pulled away from the bobbing motorboat.

Del piloted *The Turing* up the Sound. He had just spotted King's Point, when he felt the boat slow. He felt the wet on his shoes, and looked at Jess, staring at her own shoes, than looking back up at him. They were sinking.

"Jesus Christ! That thing must've cracked the hull," she said.

He looked at the shore ahead of them.

"Maybe we can make it," he said, in desperation.

It took every ounce of strength that Del had to keep his voice on an even keel. He felt as if he were being led naked to a gas chamber. He had escaped once before, all those years ago, and now, as he tempted the waters once again off of King's Point on Long Island Sound, she would hold him jealously in her clutch, squeezing the life from him as she dragged him into her realm.

They got closer to land, and *The Turing* got closer to the bottom. Within minutes, salt water washed over their ankles, and the power plant stalled. They were maybe a quarter mile from shore. Del was terrified. A moment later, *The Turing* disappeared beneath them.

"Do you know how to doggie paddle?" Jess asked, in the awkward tone of someone desperate not to humiliate.

Doggie paddle. Del was a four-time All-American in freestyle at the Academy. *Doggie paddle!*

Del suddenly forgot about the tightening grip on his chest, kicked off his shoes, slipped out of his pants, and tore off his shirt. Jess stared in disbelief.

"Come on. Hurry up," he said.

Now she was the one hesitating. But there was no choice, so she took a deep breath, and slid out of her shoes, socks and pants. She pulled off her shirt with care, even though it would never see her body again. They swam to shore. Jess, who, like most residents of City Island, had learned to swim at an early age, noticed Del's strong, easy stroke.

They slowed to a near halt when their feet touched the bottom. Del would not leave the water without seeing Jess safely on the shore first. As for Jess, the water was protecting her from Del's eyes, as she stood in her underwear, shoulder deep in Long Island Sound.

In the end, Del won out, refusing to budge, and Jess ran up onto the beach. Del followed in his soaked boxers, stroking back his hair and blowing the salty drops from his lips in relief. Jess stood, in her bra and panties, folding her arms across her chest and holding her knees together, even though it was still almost ninety degrees out with high humidity. She longed for a shower and one of her clean fluffy towels.

For the moment, the relief that Del was feeling had pushed his troubles to the back of his mind. He looked at Jess. He could see her dark pubic hair through her wet white cotton panties. He looked for an instant too long, and she blushed. She turned and walked up from the shore, arms still folded over her breasts. She was thin and in great shape, with a flat stomach, and perfect legs. He was surprised at how wide her hips were. As he followed her up from the shore, he noticed that her ass was bigger than he had expected but still very nice.

As his mind contrasted Jess's smooth tan skin with Denise's milky white glow, he wondered if his ex-wife was okay. He thought to text her but realized his phone was gone, at the bottom of the Sound, still in his pants pocket. Then he realized: his phone, that's how Spano had tracked him. He decided not to tell Jess. Then he put the thought out of his mind. There was nothing he could do. He looked up and saw the end of Pond Road and the moonlit landscape of the Bird Grove, Kings Point.

"We should try to get some sleep," said Del, suddenly feeling an exhaustion that nearly brought him to his knees.

It was almost midnight. Jess paused and nodded. She looked around and lay down on the sand. It had suddenly gotten colder, and she curled up on her side and held herself tightly for warmth. Del lay down next to her and fell asleep almost immediately. Denise crept back into his mind as he slept, and, instinctively, he reached over and put his hand on Jess's stomach, pulling her close and holding her tight. Her eyes popped open, but she didn't protest the warmth and comfort of his grip.

10

DEL WOKE FIRST and looked at his watch in the darkness. He could just barely hear the soft, high-pitched hum of the backlight as he read the numbers. He shook Jess, who started awake.

"It's almost two."

"Right," she said sitting up and yawning. "We need clothes. *Uniforms,*" she added contentiously.

She glanced around, looking unsure of which way to go.

"Come on, follow me," he directed. "It's this way."

He tried not to stare when she stood.

"How do you know this place so well?" she asked.

"I was a Midshipman."

"You went to the Academy?"

He nodded.

"Well I guess that explains why you know how to handle a boat."

She was trying not to show it, but he could tell that she was impressed.

They walked down the coast, towards a bright light about a mile down. King's Point Light, also known as the Play Pen, was actually a lighthouse that sat on top of the chapel at the Merchant Marine Academy. School lore had it that the beacon not only guided sailors safely home from the sea, but, in particular, brought the academy's midshipmen and alumni back to their alma mater from Long Island Sound.

Del remembered the first time he had climbed up into the lighthouse. He was a freshman plebe, and he brought his date, a certain Miss Kimberly Prescott, whom he had met the summer before on the docks of her South Shore country club. In trying to impress her, he wore his dress blues that night. It worked, even if they did look out of sorts as a couple—she, in her designer jeans. When he got her to the top, he showed her the beautiful view, then, as his feet shook beneath him, he moved in close, as his sophomore mentor had advised, placed his hands on her cheeks, and kissed her. He could taste her strawberry lip gloss and smell her green apple shampoo. He wondered where Miss Kimberly Prescott was now.

They didn't speak much as they walked down the beach. Jess could see that Del was caught in a daydream from the past, and she, herself, let the beautiful mansions up the bluff and the soft wet sand beneath her bare feet and between her toes take her to another world. As the salt foam washed over her feet and softened her footprints, wearing them away to soft dimples with each wave, she thought about David. She remembered the way his eyebrows wrinkled in a slightly comical expression when he smiled and the way he folded his hands behind his head when he sat at his desk at work. She thought how much he would like this moonlit beach walk at 3:30 in the morning. She decided that whatever happened, that would always be the David that she knew and remembered. That David was hers, and she would always love him.

When they got to the edge of campus, Del led the way up the bluff and onto the main green. Jess barely remembered the Merchant Marine Academy from the one time she had visited as a child with her grandfather. It was a beautiful place, resembling an oceanside country club more than a college campus. The neat brick buildings and perfectly trimmed lawns, with maritime symbols sprinkled around the grounds, leading to a boat basin at the water's edge gave a dignified yet playful air to the place. She felt a twinge of jealousy as she compared it, in her mind, to Polytechnic's institutional urban campus in Brooklyn.

As they walked along the edge of the quad, the comfort of the empty beach dissipated, and she suddenly felt exposed out in the open in her underwear, even though there was not a soul around. The campus would be under-populated during the summer, and it *was* the middle of the night, but even so, the place seemed like a ghost town. She looked at Del, on his abandoned college campus in the middle of the night in his boxer shorts, and thought how strange it must be for him. Whatever he was feeling, he didn't show it. All business, he led them right to a beautiful old mansion at the opposite end of the campus.

"The Commandant's house," Del explained.

"What if somebody's home?" asked Jess.

"He's always gone during the summer. We just need to figure out how to get in." He looked at her.

"What are you looking at me for?" she said defensively.

"Well—"

"Screw you!"

"Come on, this is no time to be touchy." He looked at the old mansion. "Maybe the windows." They were long and delicate-looking, with the imperfections of the hand of another era, beveled by time, but performing their intended function.

Always looking for the simplest solution and still not quite believing that no one would be home, Jess touched the front knob, and turned it delicately. The door opened. She looked at him as if to say, *you first*. So he headed to the entrance.

"I don't think—"

"Come on," he said, taking Jess's hand and pulling her through the open door behind him.

They walked quietly up the dark steps to the upstairs. Nothing was out of place. The master bedroom was undisturbed. The bed was still made. The plan was simple: Get cleaned up, grab a couple of uniforms, take the Commandant's car, and head to the National Lab at Brookhaven, dressed as two officers in a vehicle with a military pass. It was a good plan, and it might just work. Jess loved the idea of impersonating an officer to get in to see Lovejoy. Stealing a staff car was the icing on the cake.

Del stood guard, as Jess showered, shaved her legs, and blow-dried her hair. Despite her casual attitude about her appearance, Jesse Wolfe was surprisingly fastidious about her hygiene and personal habits. She flossed and brushed her teeth after every meal, even if it were just a light snack, and before bedtime, and in the morning. She usually showered twice a day and changed her underwear at least that often. She also changed her bed sheets every night and never used a towel more than once. She did at least one load of laundry every night.

In fact, she loved doing laundry. It was the science involved—the chemistry of it—that fascinated her. She had actually won her Westinghouse Prize by doping sodium percarbonate—a.k.a. Oxiclean, the laundry stain remover of Billy Mays infomercial fame—with carbon tetrachloride to produce a powerful, but relatively safe chemical stripping agent for fiberglass boat hulls. She failed to patent the idea and lost all the rights, but the prize panel was impressed as were her neighbors on City Island and the admissions committee at Polytechnic.

Laundry and other domestic activities were a sort of comfort for Jess. After her mother died, she took over running the house. She cooked and cleaned and did the laundry. Her quick scientific mind made culinary activities a snap. She knew how much her father loved a good meal, and she figured that was the least she could do for him after he had lost his wife at thirty-five.

She smiled as she emerged in the Commandant's monogrammed terry cloth bathrobe. Del shook his head. Jess stood guard while Del showered and shaved and laughed when he came back into the bedroom in a short, silk kimono-style bathrobe.

"Hey, this was all that was left."

"Well, no one would ever mistake you for a geisha girl."

"Come on, let's switch," he said.

She playfully gripped the bathrobe around herself and pulled back. "No way. First come, first serve."

The playful bedroom banter, as they got ready for their trip to Brookhaven, provided a welcome break from the tension, but, at the same time, there was a hidden hint of sadness for things lost or never had.

Del led Jess downstairs, through a door on the other side of the mansion, to the adjoining annex and the Academy's uniform fitting room.

"The women's stuff is on that side," he pointed with his thumb to the racks of clothing on the opposite wall.

He and Jess stood across the room from each other, facing away from one another, flipping through different sized articles of clothing. Del grabbed a black captain's uniform, which had been his last rank in the service. The 44-long jacket was still a good fit, as was the sixteen inch white button-down shirt.

"Hey, they only have skirts," said Jess.

Del turned, "Yeah, these are formal uniforms."

"I don't wear skirts."

"Well, you do today, plebe. I'm not getting busted, because you have a problem with being a girl."

His remark annoyed her, but he was right: There wasn't any choice. Besides, it was a small price to pay for being able to impersonate an officer, she told herself. She took a size eight skirt, a medium blouse, a pair of medium pantyhose, a pair of size eight shoes, and a size 7 1/8 colonel's hat into the dressing room with her. When she was done, she looked at herself in the mirror. She had to admit, the uniform looked sharp.

When she came out, Del was dressed in his full uniform, with his captain's epaulets, theater ribbons, white captain's hat, and black polished shoes.

"You look *great!*" she blurted out, surprised by her own indiscretion.

"You clean up pretty good yourself," he said. *A little flat-chested, but not bad,* he thought to himself. As his eyes moved from her body to her face, he gave her an annoyed frown. He walked over to her and took the colonel's hat from her head. He reached across and grabbed a lieutenant's hat and placed it on her head.

"Listen, plebe, on this mission, I'm the top dog."

He pinned lieutenant's bars on her shoulders, and they were ready to go.

They found the keys to the Commandant's Humvee on a peg next to the garage door. His gun cabinet was in the garage, next to his work bench, on the wall in front of the H1. The key was on the same ring. Del took two Colt .45s, an M16, a shotgun, and all the ammunition that was there.

As he loaded the SUV, Jess grinned at him, "Looks like I'm turning you into a crook." Del made a face but said nothing as they got into the vehicle, closed and locked the doors, fastened their seat belts, and headed out to Brookhaven.

They decided to play it as safe as possible and stayed off of the interstate. In fact, the interstate was clear. Traffic was thin to nonexistent all over the island, even considering that it was not yet four in the morning. It gave an eerie feeling to the drive, which made Del, without thinking, turn on the radio. The night sky gave them many more stations, but it was just more of the same. The fax-like computer tones, in particular, got on Jess's nerves. She flipped the sound system to the CD player and inserted *In The Wee Small Hours,* by Frank Sinatra.

The slot sucked the disk inside, clicked it into place, and the music played. She and Del listened in silence as Old Blue Eyes filled the car for the rest of the forty-five minute trip to the National Laboratory at Brookhaven.

11

SHE WAS SURPRISED at how many lights were on at the national lab. It was nearly five a.m., but it looked like there were more people awake at Brookhaven than on the rest of Long Island combined. They pulled to the front gate, where a military policeman stood. Del zipped down the window, as he slowed the car to a stop. The MP saw the Naval Reserves license plate, leaned down and looked at the military window sticker, saw them sitting in the Hummer, and saluted.

"At ease, Private," said Del, with a natural, but respectful, authority that both surprised Jess and made her feel protected.

The private dropped his salute and leaned into the window.

"Can I help you sir?"

"Captain Delacourt and Lieutenant Lobo here to see Professor Lovejoy at the bioengineering lab."

The MP pointed down the road. "Go straight down past the second stop light. Make a right and then an immediate left. It's the red brick building. It's marked. There'll be parking on your left."

Del zipped up his window and drove towards the lab. His smooth handling of the MP at the gate, not to mention his stone-faced use of her alias, had tickled her insides in a way that she had not felt since her grandfather played peek-a-boo with her as a child. Or maybe it was just the relief that the MP wasn't infected, wasn't one of them.

"How did you know he wouldn't ask for ID?"

"Nobody busts into a national lab wearing a Merchant Marine uniform unless they're really in the Merchant Marine."

Del parked the Hummer in the nearly empty lot next to the low, red brick building. They approached a lone marine standing guard at the entrance. He stood at attention. Del gave a salute and was about to speak, when Jess jumped in.

"At ease, Private!" she bellowed.

The marine stood at ease, looking straight ahead.

"It's Corporal, ma'am."

"Yes, right, of course," she replied, reaching for the door. The marine stopped her.

"I'm sorry ma'am, I can't let you in without proper authorization."

The marine had suspicion in his eyes, and Jess was caught off guard.

Del shook his head and looked him in the eye. "You'll have to forgive my colleague, Marine. Civilian scientists in the reserves. Don't know a goddamn thing about protocol. Damn ROTC." Del shook his head without looking at Jess.

"Yes, sir!"

"We're here to see Doctor Lovejoy." He gestured with his head to Jess. "Jesse Wolfe. And I'm Captain Delacourt."

The marine dialed on the call box next to the door.

"Captain Delacourt and Lieutenant Wolfe here to see Dr. Lovejoy."

"Yes, sir. Fine, sir." He hung up the phone.

"Someone will be up to get you shortly. You can wait inside."

The marine pushed a combination of numbers on an electronic keypad, until the lock sounded a sharp click. Del turned the knob, opened the heavy steel door, and held it for Jess.

"Thank you, Captain Delacourt," she said with a mix of sarcasm and gratitude.

Del followed her into the building. The door slammed shut with a thud and locked behind them. It was a dimly-lit entrance room, with honeycomb-reinforced beveled glass windows at either side and a steel door with a computer combination lock in front of them, on the far wall, to the left. There were brown and gold linoleum tiles on the floor. The bottom half of the walls were painted an industrial turquoise, with the top half and ceiling done in white, which had started to turn yellow with age. There was water damage in the upper right corner, above a janitor's closet. The pattern of peeling paint inside misshapen concentric loops of brown residue reminded Jess of a fractal pattern that she had once generated for a class project in high school.

She stared at the fractal rings, remembering the recursive formula that she had used to generate them, when human voices broke the silence. The first voice was low and deep and recited a long string of digits, clearly and deliberately—almost angrily—but in the distance. When it was done, a second voice, female, answered with another long sequence of digits. Del and Jess looked at each other. She had a sick feeling in her stomach.

"Don't worry, it'll be fine," said Del, his voice a little too quick to reassure her.

She took a deep breath and looked up at him. Despite the unlikely insistence, his strong demeanor actually did calm her.

Her eyes drifted to the far wall, between the janitor's closet and the combination-locked door. A restroom, unisex. As a little girl, her mother always told her to go when you can, even if you don't need to, because you don't know when you'll get the chance again. The advice stuck with her, but she wasn't about to take it now, even though the janitor's closet might mean that it was actually clean.

Her thoughts of her mother, a warm respite, were broken by more strange sounds coming from distant halls within the building: The medium-dull thud of banging metal against concrete and the still duller thud of human bone and flesh against hard inorganic material. There was a click, louder and more crisp than the other noises. It was inside the room. The knob turned on the right door, and it opened.

A medium-sized man, not quite thin enough to be frail, entered the room and approached Jess.

"Are you Jesse Wolfe?"

"Yes," Jess replied.

He forced a smile, showing his straight but gap-toothed mouth. He stuck out his right hand, and Jesse shook it. He turned to Del. They shook hands.

"Bob Lapman. I'm Professor Lovejoy's assistant."

"Is Ted not here?" asked Jess.

Surprised but not quite disapproving, Del's eyebrows went up, just in Jess's frame of view, as if to say, *Ted? She calls her advisor by his first name?*

If Bob had any thoughts on that matter, he didn't show it. He was neatly enough dressed for a scientist—slightly wrinkled button-down cotton shirt under an armless V-neck sweater, tan corduroys, and black sneaker shoes—but his slightly longish, slightly wild, thinning blond hair and his wide overly-ebullient blue eyes gave an overall appearance of entropy, rather than even dishevelment.

"He's in the middle of something, but he should be done in a little while. I'll take you down to the lab. It'll be more comfortable waiting there."

He turned and headed back though the computer-locked door. Jess and Del followed.

"As long as we have to wait, do you think we could get a tour of the place?" asked Jess.

"Good idea," said Del.

Bob looked up at nothing in particular in a moment of thought. "Um . . . I don't see why not," he said, flashing that forced gap-tooth smile that was already beginning to annoy Jess.

They walked down a long institutional corridor, with beige ceramic tiles on the walls, which gave it the look of a 1940s insane asylum. Jess thought, *another fucking idiot graduate student who thinks he's going to get something by grafting himself to Lovejoy's leg.*

Jess was one to know. She had seen them come and go before. But she knew that with her it was different. She showed up in the good professor's classroom when she was fifteen. He gravitated to her instantly. She was the brightest pupil that he had ever had. He took her under his wing. He and his wife and two daughters became like a second family to Jess. She had dinner at their house, although she always felt a little guilty whenever she left her father alone. She went shopping with his daughters at the Fulton Street Mall and did their math homework for them, until Mrs. Lovejoy found out about it and asked her to stop.

By the time she was a graduate student, she was spending more time with Lovejoy than with both of his daughters and her own father combined. She had worked out a new algorithm for factoring primes that took advantage of a design flaw in the IBM 3090 mainframe. It allowed them to decrypt passwords in minutes that had previously taken days and helped plug security holes in the NSA firewall.

He wanted her to stay to get her PhD, but she was tired of school and took the job with the CIA instead. But two years later, after the blow-up with her boss, there she was, back in Lovejoy's office, asking if his offer was still good.

By that time, he had his own lab at Brookhaven and a full professorship at Stony Brook and had his pick of doctoral students, but he could barely contain his excitement. "Of course!" he told her, delighted to have his prize pupil back, now twenty and a fully blossomed beauty.

She should have seen the signs coming. He started shaving everyday and wearing cologne. Then he started hugging her goodbye. It made her uncomfortable but seemed innocent enough, even when he rested his hands on her hips—briefly, at first, then for longer. After all, he was fifty—two years older than her father.

One day after dinner at his house, he offered to drive her home. In the car at the curb, before she had a chance to get out, he took her face in his hands and kissed her. It was the first time that anyone had ever kissed her, and, as if by some primeval instinct, she kissed him back, even though it disgusted her. She pulled back, thanked him for the ride, got out of the car, and ran inside. She brushed her teeth until her gums bled.

She hoped that the problem would go away on its own, but it didn't. The next time he tried to hug her, she pushed him away and told him that she didn't want him to do that anymore. He told her not to be hasty, but she held firm. They barely spoke after that. Despite her brilliance and her sometimes tough exterior, there was part of her that was basically a shy young girl. Lovejoy, not used to being rebuffed for anything, played the petulant child.

Then she saw the article in the *Journal of Mathematical Cryptography*: "A New Method for Factoring Primes on the IBM 3090" by T. J. Lovejoy. But the research was all hers. He had even used her examples, *knowing that she would read it*, she thought.

A week later, she left school, for good this time, and took a job with the NSA decrypting encoded cell phone calls coming from the Middle East. The director remembered her from the episode at the CIA and was glad to snag the brilliant but volatile prodigy, even letting her call her own hours and dress however she liked.

And it paid off. Her cryptanalysis helped break up one of the biggest sleeper cells in London and expose one of the major financial funding networks in the entire Middle East. She got a citation, a huge pay raise, and was put in charge of her own group at the Agency. Still, she was known as a loose cannon, with her painter's pants and t-shirts in a sea of suits, but she was too valuable to piss off, especially under the director's protection.

Then she got cocky. The fact that Lovejoy had stolen her work gnawed at her, even as she fought to suppress the memory of his wet tongue in her mouth. She was one girl who needed to get even. She hacked into the TRW network and ruined his credit. She posted his social security number on the internet. And, most devastating of all, she published a withering rebuttal to one of his most important contributions to the world of mathematical cryptography, the Lovejoy-Monte Carlo File Encryption Codec, producing a far more elegant, powerful, compact, and secure method of encrypting and decrypting files for use on networks with limited firewall protection.

Professionally humiliated with his finances in chaos, Lovejoy had a nervous breakdown. His wife divorced him. The police and then the FBI and finally the NSA, whose computers Jess had used, ended up investigating the case.

Jess was fired with cause from the Agency, indicted, convicted, and given a two-year suspended sentence. She tried to get a job in the private sector, but it was like putting a round peg in a square hole. Having been rebuffed and rejected by a system that she had done so much to help, she now worked to help those who were trapped, otherwise helpless against the bullying forces of bureaucracy.

Once she went underground, setting up her business in black market services, she became a major blogger on the dark web. Eventually, three years after her run-in with the law, she ran across Lovejoy, a.k.a. Dr. Love, through his blog. Wishing to bury the hatchet, she sent him an email. He wrote back. They spoke on the phone for a long time that first evening, both expressing remorse for what they had done.

Recovered from his breakdown, and back teaching at Stony Brook, he was still estranged from his wife and had strained relationships with both daughters. She was glad that they had spoken, and they continued to call each other now and then, but she sensed that something had gone off-kilter inside the man, and she felt responsible, at least in part. She never dreamed that he sat naked in the chair in his library, masturbating as they spoke, imagining the seventeen year old girl whom he used to spy on through a peephole in his daughters' bathroom.

Jess, for her part, felt a discomfort that she could never quite pinpoint, but part of her did care about the father figure whom she had had such an impact on, for better or for worse, and she did enjoy his fertile mind. Still, she'd only seen him once in the eight years since she'd left Stony Brook, at a brief meeting in a coffee shop almost five years ago. Hence, she was nervous as she walked down the corridor with Del at her side, behind Bob Lapman.

A dull, pounding thud snapped Jess out of her wandering thoughts. It was the same noise that they had heard in the entrance room, only now it was much louder and clear. Bob turned his head halfway back to Jess, as he kept moving forward.

"We're keeping some infected specimens in there for study."

She and Del looked at each other.

Specimens? Is THAT what they are?

Jess looked at the closed door as they walked by and wondered, *what dreams must they be having?*

Bob casually waved Del and Jess on. "If you want to observe some of the subjects later, we've got tons of them." He pointed down the hall.

An instant later, Lovejoy appeared, clutching a laptop in one hand. He emerged from behind Jess and looked at her, up and down, as she caught his moving shadow out of the corner of her eye, turning to see his sallow face smile a sort of odd, crooked smile at her.

"My god! You're in the army now!" he said.

She was shocked at how old and wild he looked. Long, gray wisps sprouted from his skull, which seemed shrunken, like it belonged to a Maori head hunter. His eyes were larger than she had remembered, with dark, creased shadows drawing to an apex at a furrow between his eyes. He seemed shorter than he used to be, although Jess was wearing pumps. Even so.

"The Merchant Marine, actually. But no, I'm not in that either." She looked down at herself in her uniform, slightly embarrassed but even more ill at ease. "It's a long story."

"Who's your friend?" He looked at Del with hungry grey eyes.

Relieved to no longer be the focus of his attention, she pointed back to Del. "This is Captain Delacourt. He *is* in the Merchant Marine." She didn't know why she lied, but Del didn't stop her. He stuck out his hand, and Lovejoy grabbed it, almost desperately, with both of his and shook it vigorously, propagating a small but perceptible percussion wave up the big man's arm and into his chest, neck, and head.

Del said nothing, but his look told Jess that he saw something amiss in the man's soul. She wanted to tell him about the toll that long hours, isolated in a lab, could take on a person's mental well-being, but she saw it too.

"Yes, yes! The military! Excellent! Excellent!"

Del took his hand from the man's clasp. He suddenly looked uncomfortable in his pilfered uniform, and it made Jess feel self-conscious in hers, even though she'd just begun to get used to it.

"Well, now that you've been on a tour of the facilities, you probably want to know exactly what we do here!" he said. Then, not waiting for an answer, he continued, "The presentation room! Yes, yes! To the presentation room!"

He walked across the lab, Del and Jess behind him, with Bob picking up the rear. They entered a large, corporate-looking room, with a long table, two white boards and a projection screen at the opposite end. He handed his computer to Bob, who plugged it into the projection system.

Del doffed his hat, carefully placing it on the table in front of him, as he sat in one of the large, comfortable boardroom chairs. Even seated, he was tall and statuesque. Jess left her hat on as she squeaked into the leather chair and crossed her legs. Lovejoy watched intently, looking at her in a lascivious way that made her remember his warm, wet tongue shoving itself into her mouth.

A flash of anger, which she had to fight to suppress, shot through her chest. *Why had she kissed him back that night in the car? Why had she bent to his will, giving him what he wanted, even if only for an instant, when she knew that it was wrong, and it disgusted her?*

"Please, relax. Enjoy the show!"

"I *am* relaxed," she said.

He smiled that crooked smile, whose asymmetry, it seemed, had changed to the other side of his face, as he stood before them. He nodded to Bob, who turned out the lights and turned on a Power Point presentation, running from Lovejoy's laptop.

Lovejoy spoke through a series of slides and graphics. He explained that prions are a type of infectious agent, unique in that they are not actually alive themselves. They are deformed proteins—the structural building blocks of all living things—and, therefore, they can potentially affect any life form that contains that particular protein.

"Usually, prion diseases, such as Bovine Spongeoform Encephelopathy, a.k.a. Mad Cow Disease, or Scrapie in sheep, or Creutzfeldt-Jakob Disease in humans are unique to that species and do not spread to any other."

He noted that prion diseases work by unraveling the physical structures involved—usually the brain—"the way a run in a stocking changes the texture and weave of the nylon," he said, echoing the line he used in his blog.

Jess could feel him stare through the darkness at her legs as he spoke. Then he turned back to the screen, which flashed a series of disturbing images and clips of people acting out violently, self-destructively, or performing odd feats of memory, cognition, and creative talent.

"Of course, once you change the brain, you change the mind."

He went on to explain that his next project would be to reverse engineer DNA in order to trace the path of human evolution, past, present, and future. He noted that ninety-nine percent of the information contained in our DNA is dormant, unused, "like a computer program waiting to be launched," he said. "By controlling the expression of this genetic information on living subjects, one would able to obtain some *interesting* results."

Lovejoy explained that initially, they had mistakenly thought that their experiments were responsible for the prions. So, he began to collect and isolate infected patients to study and experiment on, looking for a cure.

"Like human guinea pigs," said Del with disgust.

"Exactly," Lovejoy shot back with a delighted smile. His new student was catching on fast.

"The only problem with finding a cure is that prions are indestructible. They can't be killed, because they are not alive and are thus immune to all manner of toxin. They are impervious to heat and cold, and since they are just protein and contain no DNA themselves, they are even immune to radiation."

Lovejoy continued, his tone, changing from scientific to wild and dreamy.

"But then I realized that I was thinking about it all wrong. Prions aren't a disease, they're actually a blessing in disguise, the key to unlocking our hidden DNA and allowing us to live up to our full potential. They are, in fact, the perfect tool to clean out the genetic garbage from the human race and allow the elite few who survive to lead a new race, strong and beautiful and perfect."

The lights came back on. For the first time, Jess noticed what Del had probably seen the instant that they entered the room: There were no windows and only the one door, made of steel, like all the others, with the same number pad coded lock. Her mind was going a million miles per hour, as Lovejoy beamed at her.

"You know I've always loved you," Lovejoy said to her, the father, the lecherous advisor, and the mad professor all congealing to speak the truth in one pointed moment. "You and I can make this happen. Our dream. A perfect humanity."

She looked over at Del, whose stern demeanor seemed to be telling her to play it cool.

But her fear and her revulsion turned to anger, and she looked at Lovejoy with unconcealed contempt.

"You're out of your fucking mind." She uncrossed her legs and got up. "And stop trying to look up my dress!"

She looked back over at Del. "Let's get out of here."

He was already standing and putting on his hat.

Then she looked back at Lovejoy. "We're going to report you fuckers to the police or whoever else is still left and still normal."

She was about to start for the door, when she heard a noise behind her. She could see Lovejoy smile his mutating crooked smile at her.

"Hey!" Del yelled, his eyes darting behind her. Then she felt it. Bob was holding her from behind in an arm lock. She struggled, as Lovejoy zeroed in, lifting her skirt and shoving himself between her legs as he grinned manically, drool sliding in a long strand from his lower lip onto her chin.

Within an instant, Del reached across the table, grabbed Lovejoy, and pulled him off, throwing him to the ground. He brought his hand back, over Jess's head, into Bob's face, breaking his nose, but the man didn't release her, even as blood poured down his shirt. Before Del had a chance to strike again, Lovejoy was back. He turned to Jess and tried to grab her legs, but she was too quick. She pulled her knees up and kicked him in the chest full force with both heels. He went flying through the air, careening into the screen, and tumbling to the floor, his head hitting with a loud pop.

Meanwhile Del wrenched his hands under Bob's armpits and pulled him off Jess. When he finally let go of her, she dropped back into her seat and slid to the floor, her skirt riding up around her waist. Del released him for an instant, striking him hard behind the ear. His eyes rolled up into his head, and he collapsed, unconscious. Across the room, Lovejoy lay crumpled at the foot of the overhead projector. Both men now unconscious but still breathing.

Del reached down and picked up Jess. She bent over, picked up her Lieutenant's hat, and put it on, before pulling her skirt down over her legs and starting for the door. Then she stopped, something catching her eye. Lovejoy's computer, open on the floor, a large crack down the middle where he had landed on it. The screen flickered for a second, showing her a page full of symbols and equations before going black. She felt a rush through her body at what she thought she saw, but there was no time to process it. The door clicked open, and she grabbed the machine and snapped it shut.

Two men entered, blinking, mystified at the scene. Jess tucked the laptop under her arm and walked to the door with a confident stride.

"It looks like they're infected," she said, straightening her hat. "Better put them in holding."

The men stood there, looking unsure, as Jess and Del left the room.

"Hey!" a voice yelled after them, but they were already halfway down the hall. "Hey!" it repeated. "Shit! We've got a pair making a break for it!"

"Come on!" Del yelled, but Jess was already running.

They dodged two lab assistants and bowled over a man in uniform. The stairway was within sight. But then, just as they reached it, another man in uniform came out a side corridor and grabbed Jess. Del tackled him, shoved him back, and pushed her up.

When they got to the top of the stairs, Del reached for the knob, but the door was locked. He stared at the combination keypad, clueless, *trapped*.

"Out of the way," Jess said.

She pushed through, punched in the five digits, and the door clicked. Turning the knob, she swung it open and held it for Del. "After you."

He looked at her in amazement as he darted through.

"Just an old parlor trick," she said, explaining, as they ran through the waiting room, past the turquoise paint and the brown water spot on the ceiling. She could hear people scrambling up the stairs, maybe fifteen seconds behind them. Then she stopped, grabbing Del's shoulder.

"I have an idea."

She put the laptop down, turned around, and went for the janitor's closet, pulling the door open. Looking around, she struggled for what she was looking for in the semi-darkness, the sounds from the stairwell getting closer. Then she saw it: two gallons of Clorox on the floor and two more of ammonia on an adjacent shelf.

"What are you doing?!"

She turned and shoved the containers to the floor, opening them, fast and sloppy, then lunging back for the stairwell. "Ammonia and bleach makes chlorine gas," she told him, keying in the code again. "Dump it, dump it all, down the stairs, all over them!"

A second later, she turned the knob, but a hand on the other side was already there, forcing it open. Del ran over, shoved the man into the throng behind him, sending them all tumbling back down the stairs. He turned, grabbed both gallons of Clorox in one hand and both containers of Windex in the other. Jess held her breath, holding the door open, watching him balance the impossible load, while the goons on the stairs recovered and started back up. But it was too late, Del poured the whole lot down on them, pulling back, just as the cloud formed, and Jess shut the door.

She started back to the entrance, but this time, *Del* stopped *her*, picking up the laptop, straightening her uniform and then his own before leading the way outside, calm as could be. Jess followed, watching in silence this time, as Del saluted the marine, still on guard, unaware of the tumult inside.

They walked briskly to the Hummer, got in, and drove back down the road and out the front gate, saluting the other sentry. A few minutes later, they were on a dark country road, everything quiet, like none of it had ever happened.

It occurred to Del to ditch the Humvee, but that would leave them stranded in the middle of Long Island, even more vulnerable. He was lost in thought, trying to make sense of it all, when he looked over at Jess with Lovejoy's computer sitting, open on her lap, its screen dark, shattered in the struggle.

"You think you can fix it?"

She nodded. "Yeah, but I need to go back to my place on Avenue D."

He paused for a minute to consider this, finally shaking his head. "Too dangerous. We don't even know if there's anything on there."

She looked at him sarcastically.

"You can give me that look all you want, but it's a big risk, and what makes you so sure there's anything that can help us on there?"

She took a deep breath, like she was about to confess. "When we were in the room with Lovejoy, I saw something. Something flashed on the screen. It was just for a second, but—" she stopped herself, almost overcome.

Del was surprised. "What?" he asked, taking his eyes off the road to look at her.

"Like I said, it was just for a second, but I think it was a proof of the Riemann Hypothesis . . . number theory . . . really important for cryptography, musical tuning, all sorts of things." Emotion came over her face, longing and awe.

"Okay, but so what?"

"It's never been solved." She looked right into his eyes with a passion that he had not seen in her before. "Oh Del, it was so beautiful!"

He nodded, taken aback but finally understanding.

Glancing back down at the laptop, Del told her, "You know, Teddy had an Apple laptop." His eyes met hers. "My son." He looked down then back at the road.

"A 13-inch MacBook Pro?" she asked.

"I'm not sure, but it looked the same. Anyway, it's worth a try."

"Where is it?"

"My old place, downtown," he told her. Then, anticipating her next question, "Denise and I—my ex-wife—we lived there when we were married. My sister was there for a while after that, but it's empty now."

12

THE PLACE WAS NOT at all what Jess had expected. It was a medium-sized two bedroom condo in a converted pre-war municipal building, but the interior was modern and well decorated. There was a Bösendorfer baby grand in the living room, which contained a sectioned white couch and a coffee table with books on old sailing ships and the then-latest exhibits from the Guggenheim, the Whitney, and the Metropolitan Museum of Art.

There was a sleek, white fireplace which almost disappeared into the opposite wall. Sheet music for Chopin's Nocturne in B major, Opus 9, sat open on the piano's music stand. The kitchen was also white, with stainless steel appliances and Cuisinart pots hanging neatly on the wall.

As they continued through, Del led her down a hallway. There were three doors at the end, two facing; one in the middle.

"That's Teddy's room," Del said, gesturing to the door on the right. "The computer's in there."

"I need a shower," she told him.

He nodded towards the door at the end. "That's the bathroom." Then he tilted his head, weary, to the third door. "I'm going to rest for a while. Let me know if you need anything." He entered the room and closed the door behind him.

Jess put the computer down, popped off her shoes, and went into the bathroom. It was done in off-white, with a seashell theme, and it was spotless. She let the water run, as she took off her clothes. It felt good to be free of the uniform, especially the skirt and pantyhose, and she left them in a pile on the floor. A shiver of well-being surged through her body as she stepped into the shower, under the stream of warm water. Jess always did her best thinking in the shower, and normally, the events of the day would replay in her head. But there was only one thing that came into her mind now, and it would not leave.

It wasn't her mad professor, or her burned house, or even the prions themselves. All of that was shunted aside by the zeta function and the proof of the Riemann Hypothesis that she had seen in that brief flash of light. There was something otherworldly and, dare she even think it, divine about it, like the first time she had heard the eighteenth variation of Rachmaninoff's Paganini

Rhapsody, when she was a girl. As the warm water streamed over her, she reached down between her legs and touched herself, slowly at first and then faster. She never made a noise when she did this, but she grabbed the neck of the shower head hard with her other hand as her body tightened then relaxed with her soft, breathy puffs moving through the beads of water.

She left the bathroom wrapped in a fresh, terrycloth bathrobe. She could feel how clean the floor was with her bare feet as she stepped to Teddy's door. When she entered, she found herself in a little boy's bedroom.

It was unlike any other part of the house. There were hardwood floors, like in the rest of the apartment, but in this room, there was wallpaper with vintage racing cars from the '40s, '50s, and '60s. A captain's wheel with antique mariner's lights hung from the center of the ceiling. There was a bed shaped like a ship, and a small desk, with a framed picture on it.

She went over, picked it up, and looked at it. There was Del with a beautiful blonde woman and a small boy, body crumpled, in a wheelchair, smiling—or trying to— at a summer barbecue. Jess's heart sank. She could see Del's rugged good looks in his son, even through his twisted expression. It shocked her, and she wondered what was wrong with him, if he had been born this way, or if there had been an accident, or some kind of illness.

She touched her fingers to the picture, imagining Teddy in his boat-bed and at his desk and Denise and Del in the living room and bedroom. She was surprised at how fresh-faced and blonde Denise was—and how beautiful. Jess had always had a hangup about blondes. *They got all the attention*, she thought, never noticing just how many of the boys had a crush on *her*. But as she looked at Denise, she saw the appeal, and her jealousy faded.

As she put the picture down and looked for the MacBook, it never occurred to her that the little boy was dead. She found out when she saw the certificate in a pile of papers. She put her hand to her mouth as her eyes welled up. Jesse Wolfe wasn't a crier, but the thought of the little boy with the struggling smile, dead, was too much for her. A pang of grief shot through her core.

The laptop didn't turn up, but Jesse went through every drawer, wanting, almost *needing* to know what happened to Teddy. There were drawers with clothes and toys and one set full of papers. The death certificate was on top, but most of the rest were mortgage payments, bills, and piles of receipts.

Jess learned that Del's sister was named Ellen, that she was two years younger, that she wanted to be an actress, and that he had continued to pay the bills while she was living there. She found the deed to the place, Del's divorce papers, and Teddy's birth certificate. He was ten when he died. Then, she hit pay dirt. A folder from Lenox Hill Hospital.

He had a rare genetic blood disorder, an iron processing deficiency linked to the 19th chromosome. *The 19th chromosome*. And something began to dawn on her. As she piled through the papers, cross-legged on the floor, the door creaked open.

"What the hell are you doing?"

She turned, folder in hand, and looked up at Del, towering over her, still in his uniform, furious. It was the first time she'd ever seen him so angry. He strode over, grabbed the folder from her hand, and glared at her. He looked like he wanted to hit her, but he wasn't the type.

"I was just—"

"You're supposed to be working on that laptop."

"I can't find it."

"So you thought you'd just rummage through my personal life?"

"Don't be mad."

She got up and faced him. He seemed even taller in her bare feet. "My mother died from a rare genetic blood disease, just like Teddy."

His anger faded a little then re-congealed. "So what?"

"I think there may be a connection."

He shook his head, still angry. "Bullshit. What Teddy had kills you before you're ten."

She nodded, taking the chance and gently pulling the folder from under his arm, taking out the karyogram peeking out from the back and showing it to him.

"It's a different disease than my mother's, but they're both iron processing deficiencies, and they're both on the 19th chromosome." His eyes widened a little, and his anger faded. "It's too big a coincidence. I think it may be why we're both immune."

He seemed to ponder this. "Yeah, but neither one of *us* has a disease."

"No, but we're both carriers. You need two bad copies of a gene to get the actual disease, like Sickle Cell Anemia. Your son got one copy from you and one from your wife. I got one from my mother. But we're fine, because we still have one normal copy. But whatever's going on with the prions, they seem to need two good copies of that 19th chromosome to work their way in."

"So whatever killed Teddy—and your mother—has made us immune?"

She nodded. "I think so. Like Sickle Cell. Two bad copies, you get the disease and die. One bad copy, you're not only healthy, but you're immune to malaria."

They looked at each other with a kind of unspoken guilt over their dead family members, who weren't so lucky, and, in Jess's case, was subject to an internal wrath over making her a carrier.

"What about the laptop?" Del asked.

She shook her head. "Maybe your wife took it. Maybe Ellen has it."

A little surprise flashed on his face, and she realized he had never told her his sister's name. But then he nodded, taking it in stride. "Get dressed. I'm going to take a shower. Let's go down to your place and find out what's on that laptop."

She looked over at the uniform, sitting in a pile on the floor. "You have anything to wear?"

"Go into my bedroom. There's a bunch of Denise's stuff. Probably Ellen's too. Help yourself."

She hesitated then nodded, but he was already half-way out the door.

Jesse Wolfe hated wearing anyone else's clothing, but after all they'd been through, it no longer seemed like such a big deal. In fact, under the circumstances, she was glad for what she could get. So she shrugged to herself and walked across the hall into the master bedroom.

Del was already undressing, getting ready to shower, like he was in an army barracks. It made her uncomfortable, but he didn't seem to notice. She couldn't wait for him to go, but she couldn't stop herself from eyeing him as he left the room. She didn't usually notice, but he had a great body.

Jess thought about Del and his wife and how lonely she was as she picked through Denise's clothes. She had nice underwear and lots of it—enough to leave at least a dozen pairs in a place she wasn't coming back to. Jess wasn't surprised. She picked out the plainest pair she could find, white cotton briefs and a matching bra. They actually fit.

Next she went for the closet. It was a large walk-in. Like a ghost town, it was mostly empty, with only a few pieces of Del's casual clothing hanging across from a couple of out-of-fashion pants suits, a few skirts, and of pairs of old jeans. Jess imagined the two of them dressing in the morning, the sights, sounds, and smells mingling gently and hanging in the air.

She grabbed the pair of jeans and a sweatshirt. Denise was about her height but a little thinner, and her jeans were just a little tight, but the sweatshirt was a good fit. She stuffed her feet into a pair of running shoes, which were about a half size too small. Good enough.

Del walked in wrapped in a towel, looked at Jess, and grinned. "That was Denise's favorite pair of jeans."

"How come she left them?"

"Hole in the knee," he said, pointing with his eyes.

She looked down and saw the rip. Yeah, Denise didn't look like the kind of chick who'd walk around in ripped jeans.

Del started to take the towel off as he walked past Jess to the closet, and she shot out of the room. She wasn't about to watch his army barracks strip show again.

"I'm going to look for something to eat." She told him, turning her head halfway back so he could hear, as she stepped out over the threshold.

When Del came out into the kitchen, Jess had a pile of peanut butter and cracker sandwiches on a plate and two glasses of Gatorade ready on the counter.

He saw it and smiled. "Honey, you shouldn't have."

The joke bugged her, but she smiled. "It was nothing."

They scarfed it down, packing a couple of Ziploc bags for the road. Jess stuck the laptop in next to them in a canvas bag she found in the kitchen closet.

"One more thing," he told her.

He led her around the corner to the den. Whereas the bedroom was all Denise—flower patterns and pastel shades—this room was all Del. There were several judo championship trophies and photos of Del at martial arts competitions, a couple of citations for bravery, and lots of police photos. And there, under a blanket, a gun safe.

He opened it, pulled out two pistols, a shotgun, half a dozen clips, and a box of shells. He shoved them in the bag, before they got up to leave.

Jess looked at him uneasy.

He shot her an ironic smile. "It's dangerous out there."

13

WHEN THEY STEPPED out into the night, Jess was almost blinded by the celestial light show. Leaving Shelter Island, the night before last, it had been there, glowing, flickering, green and purple above the horizon. But now it was bright and brilliant, deep red, dotted by stars, lighting up the whole sky, beautiful and frightening. Del looked up into the night, slowing to a stop. She watched the light flash off his face.

"What *is* this?" he asked, turning to her.

"The Aurora Borealis," she answered. "Northern Lights."

"I've never seen anything like it."

"It doesn't usually happen this far south. Especially not in the summer. And not this big." She paused, thinking it through. "There must be a *massive* magnetic storm."

He continued looking up at the flickering red, mystified. "Where is it coming from?"

"What they call a coronal mass ejection—basically a huge explosion on the sun tearing into the ionosphere. Particles come sliding down the earth's magnetic field, get excited, give off light in different colors."

"It must've been a hell of an explosion."

She looked up, taking it in. "Yeah, I'll say. There hasn't been a show like this in a hundred years."

He looked over at her. "What the hell is going on?"

She knew what he meant, but she couldn't admit that she didn't have the answer, that she didn't know what the connection was, if any, to the prions, the madness, and the 19th chromosome. So she closed up, put up a wall, got defensive.

"I just told you."

Maybe he was distracted by the beauty or maybe he just decided to let it go, but he looked back up, breathing in deeply. "It's incredible."

Suddenly, she felt warm towards him, and regret welled up in her for her snippy comment, and she looked over at him. "I don't know, Del. I don't know what's going on. But I'm going to try to find out."

He looked at her and smiled. And there, alone with him, under the flashing sky, she wanted him to kiss her.

As they drove down to her place in the East Village, uneasy thoughts crept into Jesse Wolfe's mind. She had felt safe at Del's old apartment—there was no reason for anyone to think they'd be there. No one had lived there in almost two years. The Academy seemed safe too.

But the place on Avenue D was a different story. It was the center of her whole operation. It hadn't taken them long to find them at her place on City Island. And Spano had been there waiting at Del's timeshare on Shelter Island. The thought of it gave her the creeps.

Del pulled the Hummer up to the curb and cut the motor down the street from the building. He seemed to read her mind.

"Don't worry, we just have to get in and out quickly, that's all."

They got out of the car, and he tucked a pistol into the back of his pants. He handed Jess a .38 Police Special.

"This is the safety. Keep it on, until you need to use it. Grab the gun with both hands, like this," has said, wrapping his hands around it to show her. "Then aim for the center of your target with both eyes open and squeeze."

She nodded and slipped the gun into the back of her jeans.

The street was empty, with dirt and garbage spread everywhere. Cockroaches slithered into cracks, and rats climbed up the side molding of the building. When they entered the atrium, it was dark. The staircase echoed each step that they took on the steel-edged industrial metal stairs. The red and white paint on the two-toned walls seemed darker than usual, lit now only by the aurora's flashing red seeping in through the small stairwell windows.

And something else: numbers scrawled on the walls in dried crimson smears. Jess looked at the digits on the way up, trying to discern a pattern, but she couldn't— they seemed completely random. Staring at the lettering, she thought of Derek Remsen, his greasy blond hair, and the last time she was here.

She shuddered at the thought of his decomposing body at the entrance to her apartment, but the body was gone when they reached the top.

"Where—"

"I don't know," said Del, drawing his weapon and snapping off the safety.

He held her back, stepping into the apartment ahead of her. A moment later, he waved her in, putting his gun back in its holster. It wasn't until they moved further into the darkened apartment that they saw her: a little girl, standing in the dark, staring at them.

There was dead silence, no one speaking or even moving for the next few seconds, then Jess bent down, unsure, and forced a smile.

"What's your name?"

The girl looked at her, still silent. She was about seven or eight, pretty but deadly pale, with blond hair, wearing a white dress. Jess could see that she needed a bath.

"I think she's just scared," Jess said, looking up at Del.

"Just grab what you need, and let's get the hell out of here," Del told her. "We'll take her with us."

She wasn't sure if he was feeding her a line or not, but she went over to her closet, opened the door, and reached into the back, pulling out a laptop and a box of power supplies. She reached further in, along the bottom, until she felt her toolkit and bag of spare parts. When she pulled them out, she stood up and found herself facing two dull black holes that she could not, at first, make out in the dark.

Then she saw the smaller holes of a man's nose and the long, greasy blond hair. She dropped everything and screamed. Del turned and ran over to the closet just as the man's severed head fell to the floor.

"They're here!" the little girl screamed.

They came in from the front entrance, the back room, and the side windows. Jess recognized them. Mrs. Hernandez from 2B, running with a steak knife; Mr. Gutierrez from 4A, drooling like a mad dog, with a brick in his hand; and little Rico Sanchez, whom she had helped pass fourth grade math, with a tire iron that was almost as big as he was. Del shot two of them in the doorway then turned and shot Mrs. Hernandez in the chest, dropping her in front of Jess's desk. Jess reached for her pistol but dropped it.

"Pick up your stuff, and follow me!" he said, killing two more at the window.

She threw her MacBook and toolkit into the bag of spare parts, along with an extra power supply from the box. Then she slung the strap over her shoulder, picked up the gun, and followed Del.

They made a mad dash for the window leading to the roof, where she had fled from Del just four days before. Del emptied his pistol, shooting through the mass of prionated killers and then pulled Jess through the window and onto the roof. She struggled to hold onto the bag as she ran alongside Del.

A small pleading voice called from behind them.

"Don't leave me!"

Jess turned and saw the little girl standing in her white dress, terror in her eyes, as Mr. Gutierrez and others grabbed at her. Del stopped, looked at Jess and followed her eyes to the little girl.

"I'm going back," she said, but Del stopped her.

"I'll get her."

He ran back through the window into the apartment, like a fireman into a burning building. He tore the pawing hands from the girl's face and body, picked her up, tucked her under one arm, and ran back to the window, passing her through to Jess before stepping back out onto the roof. The three of them ran across the roof and descended the creaky, rusted fire escape, hands and eyes reaching out at every level, until they reached the sidewalk.

When they got to the car, a man was standing on the hood with a crowbar, and two more were coming down the street from behind. Del snapped in a new clip and shot the man on the car dead. He tumbled off to the ground as Del backed the Hummer out from under him, running over another one in the process. They sped west on 10th Street, along the north side of Tomkins Square, the three of them crammed into the front seat.

"They were waiting for us. They knew we'd come here eventually. They were just waiting and watching until we showed up. And we did exactly what they expected," Jess said, disgusted at herself. "Where the fuck do we go now?"

Del looked down at the little girl, seated between them, and then up at Jess.

"I don't know, and watch your mouth," he said.

She looked at him, annoyed. "Yeah, okay. So where the *heck* do we go now?"

"We could go back to the apartment."

Jess shook her head. "They'll figure that out too." She looked almost sullen. "If they haven't already."

It only stood to reason. The eyes looking out from the darkness of her place on Avenue D were patient, methodical, and coldly logical. They'd connect all the dots eventually. She wasn't going to be outsmarted again. The three of them needed to find somewhere else. And fast. Then she thought of something.

"I know a place," she said.

14

THEY LEFT the Hummer at St. Mark's Place and Avenue A and headed south, towards Houston Street, carrying their stuff. They crossed the desolate thoroughfare, stepping over bodies, debris, and things unidentifiable in the darkness of Essex Street. Jess led them deeper into the maze of the Lower East Side, taking them down Rivington, past a faded sign for Schapiro's Kosher Wine, and a Chinese Laundromat, around an unlit corner, to a looming abandoned edifice.

The Synagogue on Ludlow Street had been there for well over a hundred years but had been abandoned since at least the 1970s. Its Romanesque façade of orange brick was cracked and swelled with moss and water damage. The giant stained-glass Star of David had more than half its panes missing or broken, and the smaller windows, including two arched concrete vaults on either side of the giant double front doors, were boarded up entirely. Below the Hebrew lettering above the archway, there was a sign in Chinese and English promising conversion to a Confucian temple.

Del hoisted himself up past the cornerstone, reading 5645, to the window ledge. He punched his hand through the rotten plywood and squeezed between the rusty nails to enter the building. Jess passed the little girl through, and then Del helped her, at last, into the building.

The inside was dark, but the flickering aurora gave an odd sort of light show through the remaining stained glass windows. The pews were scattered with Hebrew prayer books, collapsed beams, moldy plaster dust, and fallen roofing.

"How did you know about this place?" Del asked, looking around at the broken interior of the once-great house of worship.

"My great-great-grandfather built it. Or had it built. I used to come here when I was a kid to throw rocks though the windows."

"I thought you lived up on City Island."

"Yeah, well, my grandfather lived down here. The place on Avenue D actually belonged to *him*. *His* grandfather was some big rabbi from Romania."

"I thought you were some kind of blue-blood WASP."

"Only on my dad's side."

Del furled his eyebrows in an almost mocking expression. "Let me guess, that rabbi from Romania, he wasn't Rabbi *Wolfe* by any chance?"

Jess gave him a facetious grin. "You're pretty smart, Delacourt. You ought to be a detective."

Del gave no response but flashed the self-satisfied look of a bear that had just found a pot of honey.

"Anyway," Jess said, "they'll never look for us here."

Jess sat on the edge of the *bima*, laying her tools, both laptops, and two extra batteries beside her. She removed Lovejoy's hard drive and installed it in her own machine, swapping hers out and clicking his battery, which she guessed was fully charged, in place. She had everything back together and booted up within twenty minutes.

Del said nothing, glancing over at her periodically, as he cleaned and reloaded his gun and extra clip. It got on her nerves, but she relaxed once the machine came to life. Then, when she tried to access Lovejoy's drive, the operating system stopped her, asking for a password. Del continued to watch, actually coming over, as she rebooted in UNIX and removed the password protection, bypassing the Apple security. When she brought the machine back up, the password was gone, and the professor's file system was sitting in front of her.

"I guess that password wasn't too secure," he said.

"None of them are."

He continued looking over her shoulder, peering in closer.

"Do you mind?" she said, looking back over at him holding the pistol like a little boy with a toy gun.

"Yeah, no problem," he told her.

Still looking up, she watched him re-holster his gun, chastised, and it made her feel bad. *Men don't like bossy women*, she thought.

"I just need to dive into this on my own for a while," she said, trying to soften it. Meanwhile, she noticed that the little girl had wandered into the seating area, walking through the pews. Looking out at her, she gestured with her head. "Maybe you can find out her name or something."

Almost immediately, Jess regretted the last two words, *or something*. It made it seem like she was dismissing him, which she was, but she didn't want him to think that. *Men don't like it when you're smarter than they are either*, she thought. She'd definitely been *there* before—being too smart, or too smart-mouthed, scaring men off, wrecking first dates and first conversations.

But he seemed to understand—she just needed to be alone while she worked, that's all. And he went down into the pews to the girl, started talking to her as she sat, flipping through one of the ancient Hebrew prayer books. It was okay.

She barely heard his voice, as she went through the directories and files. She needed to find out what Lovejoy had figured out, what had happened at the lab, what was going on with the prions. But there was something else she looked for first: any trace of the Riemann zeta function; anything, anything at all that might lead her to a proof of the famous hypothesis. There was nothing.

Exasperated, she looked out at the synagogue, at Del and the little girl. He was carrying her, asleep, back up to the bima. When he got to the edge where she was sitting, he stopped.

"How's it going?" he asked.

"Okay," she lied.

She looked at the little girl, dead to the world, in Del's arms. "So what's her name?"

"Don't know. She isn't talking."

Looking closely, Jess noted for the first time just how gray her pallor was. "She doesn't look good. Is she okay?"

"I think she had lead poisoning. I see it sometimes. Kids eat paint chips in older buildings. It builds up in their bodies."

Jess thought of the paint bubbling off the walls in her building on Avenue D, but she didn't want to believe it. "Are you sure?"

"Yeah." He pushed open her mouth, showing a blue line along the base of her teeth. "Accumulation on the gums. Dead giveaway." He tilted his head toward the far side of the synagogue. "She peeled some of the paint off the back wall, tried to eat it, before I stopped her."

Her concern must've registered on her face, and Del sought to set her mind at ease. "Don't worry, she'll be okay," he reassured her. "It'll wash out of her system eventually."

She watched him walk up the steps and lay the girl down, still fast asleep, by the pulpit. "I'm going to sleep for a bit too," he told her.

She wondered if the girl really would be okay, where she was from, and where her mother was, but she didn't have time for it.

Looking back at the screen, she knew she had to find the professor's notes; she had to find them if there was any hope at all. But she had to admit, it *did* seem hopeless, and she wondered if they were all just doomed. Watching Del and the little girl sleep, she wanted to curl up between them, but she couldn't. They were depending on her. Other survivors were depending on her. *She* was depending on *herself*.

So she dug back through the files. She hadn't seen anything that looked remotely like a logbook the first go-round, but Lovejoy was an odd duck: he had his own way of reasoning, and Jess knew he was unlikely to use a straightforward filing system. But she was sure it would be there. At least that's what she told herself. She found it in a directory named after his dog, Donny. Jess remembered Donny from her days at Polytechnic, and the thought of the little brown mutt made her smile. The happy moment was brief, as she read through his notes, almost four hundred pages worth.

It started simply enough. Lovejoy had won a government research grant to extend the Human Genome Project by sequencing heterochromatic parts of human cell DNA, which had not yet been mapped. He finished so far ahead of schedule that he began to study the results in more detail, delving into parts of this code and others that were recessive, masked, or otherwise suppressed.

Mapping the base pairs and examining blood samples, he noticed a certain anomaly cropping up, just a few times at first, then more and more frequently. A rogue protein. *It had to be coming from our own DNA.* But with 23 chromosomes and three billion base pairs and no known function to map, he had no idea which gene, which part of which chromosome caused the prions. So he set it aside, finishing the project and forgetting about the misshapen proteins.

But then the outbreak happened.

He began to think about the prions he had found. After isolating some tissue samples, his suspicions were confirmed: prions—rogue, misshapen proteins—were responsible. He couldn't figure out how it had happened, at first thinking that maybe *he* was even responsible, but he quickly realized that it was much bigger than his work in the lab. He was a witness, not the cause. And then, he began to realize, he was becoming a victim.

He searched frantically for the cure or at least some way to fight it. He felt certain that the answer lay somewhere in our genetic code. *Our genes*, he wrote, *trace not only our evolutionary past but also our future.* Jess read on, in horror, as he described catching sight of himself in the mirror, late one afternoon. There was blood around his mouth. He couldn't understand it. Then, looking around, he saw a pile of intestines lying at his feet and a woman, dead, eviscerated, nearby. He could taste her blood and bile in his mouth, and he liked it.

Still clinging to some remnant of sanity, he knew he didn't have much time if he was going to find a cure.

Then he had an epiphany. *The prions weren't a contagion or a disease: They were a tool, a part of the evolutionary process, used to unleash our genetic code, change our brain structure, and move us forward. The prions were good, he decided.* And, for the first time, it became clear to Jess that the prions were not only altering brain structure but also altering—*reprogramming*—our DNA.

Lovejoy delved further into our genetic code, as he descended into madness. He left the message for Jess: He needed her fine mind to decrypt the masked sequences. He wanted her to join him "on the next level." And that was where the log book ended, the day before last.

She closed the laptop, stood up, and looked around. The sun had already been up for a while, but Del and the little girl were still asleep. Once again, she wanted to join them, but she was wide awake.

Undistracted and with daylight pouring in through the stained-glass windows and open holes, she finally took the place in, in all its detail. It was filthy and ruined not quite beyond repair, but she could tell that it had once been magnificent. The bima stood tall above the main seating area. The eternal flame, now extinguished, crowned the empty ark with its Hebrew lettering that she could not understand. Around the inside perimeter, above the main seating area, was the women's gallery. *Women's gallery my ass*, she thought. But still, the face of the open, rectangular balcony, decorated with biblical frescos in darkened shades of spectral pigments, made her marvel.

As many times as she had seen this building, this was the first time that she had ever been inside. Her grandfather had taken her, on an irregular basis, to the synagogue on Pike Street, until she was seven or eight. Then he died, and her father decided that she should be raised a Methodist. She hated getting dressed up for Sunday services but liked the people in the congregation on City Island. She never took to religion, though, and, to this day, resented the death of her mother too much to let herself believe.

Even so, the mysterious Hebrew letters sent a chill through her as she looked at them, under the darkened flame, through the stale summer air of the old synagogue. As she went to find a place to pee, she remembered the passage from Exodus, where God tells Moses to take off his shoes, because he is standing on holy ground.

As she squatted in a dark corner, two eyes peered out at her. She gasped in a moment of terror. It was just the little girl, but the shock sent an epigastric surge through her solar plexus, and, in a long instant, she saw the day the synagogue opened.

There were women in long dresses, with their heads covered and men, with yarmulkes and long beards. One tall, handsome man with her same green eyes and her mother's smile shook hands with the rabbi. He looked through her and spoke words that she did not understand. The desolate building re-emerged, and Jess pulled herself back together, unable to finish.

She looked at the little girl with a deep hunger to know.

"Jess?" Del's voice boomed from the bima, taking her attention.

"Yeah, over here."

She came out of the darkness and told him everything in the professor's log. They finished the rest of their food, feeding the little girl, who was still silent. Although she tried not to show it, Jess was increasingly grieved at the plight of her professor, a man who had had such an influence on her and for whom she held such intense mixed emotions. She wondered how his daughters were doing, but it was too much for her to even think about it.

By the time she was done, the daytime sun had faded into afternoon light. Finally in position, it shone directly through the great Hebrew seal, the Shield of David, until it disappeared, leaving the empty house of worship draped in night once again. Within minutes, the aurora emerged, still bright, now dark green.

"If I can find the exact sequence of DNA that makes this protein, transcribe it, reconstruct the prion molecule—virtually, that is—then I can figure out how to destroy it," Jess said, standing over Del, sitting on the edge of the bima, projecting more confidence than she had any right to.

"Without killing us in the process, I hope," Del added.

Jess was annoyed. He was being negative and just not *getting* it. "The point is I can reduce it to a problem of gene prediction, bioinformatics, *cryptography*. I just need to take all the base pairs for the human genome—we've got them on the laptop—and find that sequence."

He looked up at Jess. "But if *the professor* couldn't do it with a whole lab at Brookhaven, how are *you* going to do it in an abandoned temple with a Mac laptop and nothing to eat?"

She hated the way he emphasized *the professor*, like he was somehow smarter than she was, but she put it out of her mind. It was nothing personal. But he *still* wasn't getting it. She'd just have to slow down and explain it to him. "Look, the human genome contains three billion base pairs on 23 chromosomes. It might take six months to find the right sequence, even with the computers at Brookhaven. But *I* know it's on chromosome 19. That reduces the amount of data to cull through by 98 percent. That's still millions of base pairs to decrypt, but it's doable," she told him, pausing. "With both laptops running in parallel, it shouldn't take long to find the exact sequence. A few days maybe." Then she added, almost as an afterthought, "I just have to write a program."

She was worried that he would question her ability to come up with the right code-cracking program on the fly, always an iffy proposition, as she watched him sitting on the edge of the bima, thinking. But he asked something else.

"Are you really that sure it's on that 19th chromosome?"

She looked at him like he was an idiot, but she had to be patient. She needed him. He had to be convinced, or they—and any other survivors—were done for. "We're both carriers of rare genetic diseases linked to that chromosome, and we're both immune to the prions. The odds of that being a coincidence are about one in a hundred million."

"Wow, really?"

She'd made the number up, though she was certain that the odds were at least that high. Not wanting to give him a chance to reconsider, she quickly added, "And I even know it's on the same *gene* within that chromosome, because they're both iron storage diseases."

He nodded in agreement, but then a stray thought seemed to enter his head. "But what exactly triggered this gene on chromosome 19 to go haywire all of a sudden?" he asked. *"In everybody all at once?* I mean, it's supposed to be controlling our iron metabolism, and then, all of a sudden, it's reprogramming us."

It was a hell of a good question, and she wasn't expecting it. She looked around, trying to think of something to say. His eyes followed hers to a stained glass window above the women's gallery, both of them staring at the aurora flashing through the translucent image of the finger of God touching life into Adam.

"Don't magnetic fields affect iron?" he asked.

Her mouth hung open, through a long, still pause that seemed to change everything.

Del finally broke the silence with the most base and mundane call imaginable. "I'll be right back," he said, as he turned and started for the same dark corner that they had been using as a latrine all day.

"Del?"

"Yeah?"

"Could you do that outside?"

He stopped walking and turned back to her. "Sure, of course."

15

JESS WOLFE pretended she was used to roughing it, but the truth was she needed a more comfortable place to work, a clean bathroom, and a change of clothes. And something to eat. They were out of food. She worried about the little girl. Del seemed to read her mind, telling her about a new housing development north of the city, in Westchester, that he and Denise had looked at, before it was even built. It was a semi-rural, upper middle class suburban community, with woods, and streams, and fresh air for Teddy. They never bought that house on the cul-de-sac, but Del had received a notice in the mail three weeks ago announcing that the houses were nearing completion, with a couple of units still available.

"They're not even finished yet. There'll be nobody there—totally empty," he said, a note of hope in his voice.

It was a risk, but they decided to go. They left the Hummer and grabbed another car—no point in taking extra chances. Jess hotwired a Ford Taurus. It even had a full tank of gas. The city was eerie but not quite menacing, like a house that's too big for the family that lives there. They decided to take side streets—less chance of being trapped, though there weren't many people around, and the few that were didn't seem to pay them any attention.

"Not that I'm complaining, but one minute, everyone's after us, the next, they don't even know we're here," Del said.

"Because they're not expecting us here," she said. "But it doesn't matter to them. They're patient, systematic. They know we'll turn up, eventually. Like someone on the most wanted list."

They looked at each other, and Jess, realizing what she had just said, laughed. "I guess you got me on that one," she told him, leaning back in her seat. "But don't tell me that crime doesn't pay."

She wanted to say more, opening her mouth for an instant, to tell him how glad she was that she was with him, that they'd met, that at least if they had to go through this, they could do it together, but she stopped herself. It was an awkward moment, but it made her smile.

A fire, burning on a street corner, like an urban cookout, broke her grin. The smell was savory and rich. She put it out of her mind, even though she was sure she knew what it was.

As they wound through the streets of Manhattan, more people and other strange sights, less violent, but no less disturbing than they had seen a few days before, came into view. Bodies being stacked and cleared like cordwood. People scrawling numbers on walls and sidewalks, talking, nodding, with bodies nearby. And violin players, always, someone, on the violin.

"Don't look," Del told her. "It's like I'd tell my men in the war. Just get where you're going. Do your job. Don't pay any attention."

She tried, but her eyes took it all in. She could see that Del did too, despite his advice. Only the little girl seemed oblivious. There appeared to be people who were giving orders, and others obeying them. And those dead bodies. Jess could hardly stand it. Then, when they entered the upper part of the island, north of Central Park, the streets seemed empty again.

The aurora was still there, bluish-green, and she thought about the light coming through the synagogue.

Right on cue, Del looked over at her. "So why'd you come down to throw rocks through the windows?"

"Huh?"

"You said when you were a kid, you'd come down to the temple and throw rocks through the windows."

"I don't know. I guess I was mad. You know, they feed you all this bullshit about God, and then your mother dies."

"Then why'd you tell me not to piss in the temple?"

"I don't know. Leave me alone."

There was a long pause, then Del said, almost to himself, "There are no atheists in foxholes."

"Yeah, well, meet your first one."

She was tired and hungry and wanted a shower, but she was girding for a fight. "If you think the last few days have made me believe in God all of a sudden, you must be an idiot."

"Hey, relax," he told her, gesturing with his hands. "I'm just making conversation."

She didn't respond, happy to let it go. But there was no respite, as her mind went to the vision of her great-great-grandfather at the opening of the synagogue and to the Riemann zeta function that she had seen in a flash at Brookhaven. Maybe it really was some weird religious vision, but Jess's mind was too logical for that.

She knew that seizures sometimes manifested themselves as hallucinations. Seizures were also symptomatic of disease, for example, the disease that killed her mother. Maybe they were symptomatic of prions warping your brain too. She didn't know, but she wanted to tell him, to let him know, to warn him, but she didn't dare. Then that smell, much stronger, wafted in, taking her attention.

They were on Broadway, nearing 168th Street—New York–Presbyterian Hospital. As they passed, both their heads turned at the sight: workers hauling bodies into something that looked like an incinerator, with others directing them. The contraption, a large, sectioned off portion of the old, stone hospital, was connected by a series of cables and scaffolding to what looked like a power plant under construction.

"Is that—"

"Yeah," Jess interrupted, not wanting him to finish the sentence, not wanting to hear what they both could see: they were using people as fuel.

Jess stared. It looked like some kind of reactor core that ran on human flesh, hooked to a turbine generating electricity. The smell didn't seem to bother them. Neither did the task. It was efficient and clever, and Jess had to hold herself in check. She did long enough for them to clear the plant.

"Pull off," she gestured.

She didn't need to tell him why. Del took the Ford down 172nd Street and pulled over to the curb. Jess opened the door, leaned out, and vomited. Hanging her head down over the curb, she paused, breathing, in and out, before more came up. When she was done, turning back into the car and shutting the door, Del was there with a handkerchief. She wiped her mouth and looked at him with sad eyes.

"I'm sorry," she said.

He shook his head, dismissing her need to apologize. Eyes straight ahead, he turned the car around and put them back on course, not saying another word. It was kind of him, but she could tell from his stony expression that he felt it too. He had just seen it before—death, that is. In the army, on the job.

His emotionless face said it all, how it weighed on him, how he'd learned to deal with it, how he'd never get used to it. For the first time in her life, she appreciated what it must be like on the other side of the law, to be a cop or a soldier, and she regretted some of the things that she had done in her life. But there was no time. Now, all that counted was what she did next.

They continued north, past the Cloisters and the park, with its old forest trees, outcroppings of Manhattan schist, and secret caves, carved by glacial ice in the last eon, and used, in another time, by the Lenape tribesmen who once lived on this part of the island. Jess could see the subway yard off to the right, silver cars sitting, waiting, like everything was normal, just before they crossed the water.

Going up Riverdale Avenue, through the Bronx, past West 261st Street, and into Yonkers, they tracked the Hudson River through Dobbs Ferry and Irvington. The landscape appeared normal, but then it would shift. More bodies, someone being killed, an oblivious bystander, a number scrawler. All against a backdrop of tree-lined streets or an outdoor shopping plaza or a highway overpass.

It was almost midnight when they reached Sleepy Hollow. Turning down Old Hollow Road, Del found the entry to the development, nestled in the trees. The woods obscured the aurora, softening the light to dark, minatory shades of green and yellow. Jess felt butterflies in her stomach as the car ground and popped down the unpaved road to the cul-de-sac at the end. When Del cut the engine, they sat for a moment in silence.

"Let's go in. It doesn't look like anyone's here," he said.

Or maybe they're waiting for us, she could almost feel him thinking.

16

WHEN DEL SAW the cluster of houses in the clearing, he remembered that day with Denise and Teddy, almost four years before, when they drove up to look at the empty lots. The tract of land had been part of a private estate, belonging to a construction magnate who had lost his fortune by underestimating the cost to build a new stadium in Charlotte, North Carolina.

Del remembered thinking how this would be a great place for Teddy to grow up, a country home, still close enough to the city for him and his wife to commute. He thought of his boy, now dead, and Denise, fate unknown. Only *he* was here now, walking towards that now-cleared land, dotted with that patch of houses, Jesse Wolfe, a.k.a., Jessica Sweet, and an unidentified blonde girl in tow. He saw "For Sale" signs on some of the lawns. All but one had "Sold" pasted over them.

Del scoped out a large brown-shingled house at the end of the cul-de-sac. It was one of the ones that was sold, and it looked ready to be moved in to.

"That one," he said, pointing the way.

It was dark, and Del felt uncertain as he tried the front door. *Locked.* But there was a realtor's key box looped around the knob.

"Want me to give it a try?" Jess asked, apparently resigned to her role as group criminal.

But Del held her back, noticing for the first time that she was carrying the little girl, who was resting her head against Jess's shoulder. He took it in for a split second before turning back, pulling his gun, and breaking the key box open with a single shot. A few seconds later, he opened the front door and entered, gun still drawn.

"Anyone here?" he yelled.

Walking in deeper, he waved Jess in, satisfied that the place was empty.

The house was big but well laid-out, with a central living room giving access to the kitchen, powder room, and master bedroom with attached bathroom. The second floor had three more bedrooms, two more bathrooms, and an upstairs den.

It still smelled like paint, and although the house was not complete in some minor details—missing fuse box cover, an unhinged door, a few missing pieces of trim—it was ready for occupancy. In fact, a white sectional couch, the master bed, and much of the furniture were in place. And there were boxes piled in the main rooms and in the bedrooms for the new owners who were destined never to arrive. Del could see from the bill of lading that the clothing and personal affects had arrived and were ready to be unpacked.

Jess flicked the lights and turned on the kitchen sink. Everything was hooked up and working. She put her head under the faucet and took a drink of water, savoring its spring minerals as it washed down her throat. She flipped on the garbage disposal just for good measure. A rush of excitement went through her arms as she reached for the door to the refrigerator. She pulled it open and was met by a stream of cold air. It was nearly empty, but there was a case of Coke on the bottom shelf and a brown paper grocery bag with a note pinned to it: *Thought you might be hungry after your long trip. –S.*

Jess poked through the bag: Sandwiches, coleslaw, potato salad, and pickles. None of it was fresh anymore, but it would do. They ate at the kitchen counter. Jess was always picky about her pastrami, eating only the extra-lean cuts from Katz's on Houston Street. She wasn't complaining now, though, eating slowly and deliberately, savoring every stringy bite. Del ate his faster, finishing each half in three or four bites, almost taking the tip of his finger with the last chomp. The little girl took longer, but Jess was glad to see that she finished.

They looked through the boxes. There were books, papers, clothes, jewelry, and other personal affects. There were also several boxes marked *kitchen*, containing not only pots, pans, silverware and the like, but also food—non-perishables like tuna, beans, rice, and sugar.

"Looks like we have everything we need," Del said.

Jess looked at him for a long moment, wondering exactly what he meant. In that instant, she decided she never wanted to leave this place. Then she opened the box with photos of the family who had purchased the house.

They were a couple in their late thirties with a boy and a girl, who looked to be about eight and ten. He was a civil engineer, and she was a psychologist. Normally, Jess would have held such conventional people in contempt. But now she could only feel pity in her heart for the family whose dreams had been liquidated by a soulless horde of misshapen proteins with no more conscience than a steel beam.

"They look like nice people," she thought out loud, as she held a family photo delicately in her hands.

Del glanced over and saw. "Yeah."

Jess thought about Del and his family, but she didn't allow herself to dwell there, for his sake as well as her own. And so, she snapped back. She had a job to do. And she was the only one who could do it. But first things first.

"I need a shower," she said to Del. "And she needs a bath," she added, tilting her head to the little girl.

They all smelled horrible, and Jess, for one, had difficulty concentrating in such a state. She took the little girl to the upstairs bathroom. She drew a warm bath for her and took off her shoes and socks, and the now foul white dress and underwear. As she bathed her, washing her long blond hair, the little girl smiled. It was just a little smile, but it made Jess feel warm inside.

She wrapped the girl in a fluffy towel and disappeared into her own shower, melting into the clean, hot water. The number scrawlers crept into her head. Since she was little, she'd had a photographic memory for numbers, and one particular sequence that she'd seen on the way up was familiar. She couldn't place it, but she knew she'd seen it before. It troubled her as she dried off and put on pajamas that she'd found in one of the boxes, but she was so tired, she could hardly think enough to worry about even one more thing.

The three of them slept in the master bedroom, the little girl between Jess and Del. She desperately wanted her own space, but she didn't dare. Too dangerous. Del made her feel safe. And she wanted to keep the little girl close. Before her mind had a chance to think of anything else, she was asleep.

Despite everything, J. Samuel Delacourt, Jr. had the blank dreams of a warm summer evening, quiet and peaceful. Jesse Wolfe, however, spiraled through a maze of scenes and images that gave silent voice to the empty torment of her worst fears.

She found herself standing on a long concrete slab pier on the South Brooklyn waterfront. She was naked and felt the vulnerability of prying eyes. She scanned the post-apocalyptic industrial wasteland of the football field–sized piers, but there was no one, only a giant warehouse filled with salt. She could hear the water splashing underneath, and she could see Red Hook, where she had once thought about getting her own apartment with two other students, protruding into Upper New York Bay. Lower Manhattan was a faint, dreamy image, bleeding through the hazy mist of the gray autumn day.

Jess could feel the cold on her body. She used to come down here, to the water's edge, and watch the container ships amidst the solitude and stillness of the smokestacks and warehouses. There were no container ships now, only the pier and the water beyond. She walked to the end, acclimatizing but not quite getting used to the chill in her bones. She looked down at the dark green water and felt a force push hard against her. She had no time to look back as she flew off the pier and plummeted into the cold dirty waters of the bay.

She gasped, sucking in a mouthful of the foul water that now completely enveloped her. She was not a strong swimmer, but she pulled her head up above the water and began to doggie paddle. She looked back at the pier, which was now, somehow, at least thirty yards away. It loomed overhead, in a way that she had never before realized from her perch standing above the water. Someone or something had pushed her—she was now in the water—but she saw no one and nothing on the pier.

Yet she knew something was there. She felt it, now, in the water with her. Doom and panic hit, and she swam as fast as she could, away from the pier, towards the land across the bay. The tanks of an oil refinery congealed out of the fog. She swam and swam, until, suddenly, she was on the shore. She collapsed in the dirty sand, which stuck to her salty,

sticky skin. She stood. There was sand in her hair and be-
tween her legs. She felt something wrap around her chest,
like a concrete pillar.

She opened her eyes, awake, breathing hard. Daylight cast a spider web shadow through the paned-glass
window. Jess slowed her breathing, taking in deep lung-
fuls of air. She felt her body, miraculously free of grime
and sand, warm and dry. Del's eyes opened, and he
stretched his arms, savoring a last yawn.

Chest bare, he looked at her. "Bad dream?"

She didn't answer, but the little girl was awake now too.

"I'll get us some breakfast," she said finally.

"No, I'll take care of it. You've got work to do."

17

JESS SET UP shop in the downstairs living room, the girl playing at her feet with a doll, clearly used, until recently, by another. In her new pajamas, she sat on the couch, sideways, legs folded under her, laptop touching her knees as she typed away. Del looked at her. Her longish hair, wild from the night, laying against the pink flannel PJs made her look like some kind of cult figure or maybe the chick-geek version of an Indian guru. *Jessica Sweet*. He shook his head. He'd spent months tracking her down.

He came over and put a bowl of vegetable soup on the coffee table next to her. She looked up.

"Sorry, kiddo, we're all out of eggs."

He realized a second too late that *kiddo* probably wouldn't go over too well, but she smiled at him anyway.

"It's perfect. Thanks."

"I'm going to check out the other houses, look for more food," he told her. Then he pulled out a .38, put it down on the coffee table, next to the soup. "It's cleaned and loaded." He handed her a two-way radio, as he held up a second one. "I found these with the movers' equipment. Call me if you need anything." He strapped on a second pistol, police-style, in a harness holster around his chest and headed out.

Normally, Jesse Wolfe would have been glad to be left alone with her computer and a problem to solve, but when she heard the door shut, she felt cold and empty and more than a little afraid. Looking down at the head of blond hair, she was grateful for the little girl.

"Want some soup?"

The girl turned, and Jess forced a smile, unfolded her legs, and sat the girl on her lap. They shared the bowl, Jess feeding her the last several spoonfuls, and the girl spoke. "Thank you, Mommy."

Jess froze, not knowing what to say or do, finally telling her, "Okay, Sweetie. Go play with your dolly. Mommy has work to do."

The girl went back to her doll, and Jess went back to her computer. She puzzled over how to isolate the correct sequence of DNA and reconstruct the prion, the rogue protein that she would need to destroy. Her gut sank, and a wave of panic hit her. She was smart, and she knew where to look, but the problem suddenly seemed hopeless to her.

She made herself a cup of hot water. On the third sip, it hit her. She had all of the DNA sequences from the human genome project from *before* the prions hit right there on Lovejoy's hard drive. And she had the sequences that he had mapped from *after* the infestation in another directory on the same drive. And she already knew roughly where the problem was.

It was true that there would be other mutations by now, lots of them. But the professor had done his mapping early on, just at the start of the trouble, so that maybe there would only be a few mutations beyond the source. And maybe, just maybe, on that lonely stretch of that 19th chromosome, just the one, the lynchpin. She just had to compare the before and after samples for that segment of the 19th, look for where there was a big difference. With any luck, there would be just one, and that would be the culprit.

But she still needed a way to compare them, quickly, efficiently, automatically, and without error. She thought about DNA, the double helix, wound in long strings of nucleotides, base pairs of four distinct molecules: adenine, guanine, cytosine, and thymine. The long sequences of these base pairs map directly to every structure and metabolic process in our bodies, determining exactly who and what we are.

She thought of the four chemicals. A, G, C, and T. Like four digits. And *that* hit her too. She could model the sequence as a base-4 number—quaternary—converting it easily to base-10, octal, hexadecimal, or binary. *Binary* . . . zeros and ones. The ultimate machine code. Once she had it in binary—a string of ones and zeros, on-off switches, her computer could compare them through direct logical operation on its own internal memory. XOR, an exclusive logical disjunction, would yield the corrupted string, fast and efficient.

She wrote the program in an hour. It would have taken even less, but she'd made an error, a typo, and it took her twenty minutes to track down the bug in her code. When she finally ran it on the data from the 19th chromosome, one sequence popped out, just like she'd hoped. It was on the same part of the gene that produced ferritin, a key protein for regulating the metabolism of iron in the human body.

And there it was: human DNA, reduced to a series of numbers, then the pure logic of a machine applied, courtesy of the oversized brain of one Jesse Wolfe. She'd still have to figure out how to destroy it, but Jesse Wolfe grinned from ear-to-ear. This part, at least, she had solved.

She wanted to tell Del, but he wasn't back yet. She looked down. The little girl was gone too.

18

DEL WENT THROUGH each of the houses, gun out, ready for anything. They were all quiet, but in a creepy way, in various stages of near-completion. Some did not yet have bathroom fixtures or lighting; others were not yet painted; two of them had boxes and moving supplies. Del read the labels: *George's Bedroom, Dave's Room, Den, Living Room, Denise's Stuff.* Denise! His eyes widened for a second. He opened the box. It belonged to a teenaged girl named Denise. There was a picture of her with her friends and another with her mom and what looked like her sister. He found a Post-it note that read: September 21—driving test! Hooray! There was a smiley face, and the i's were dotted with tiny hearts. He put it back and went to the kitchen.

In the refrigerator was another bag from the same deli with the same note from the same realtor as the one they'd found in their own, the previous day. Del couldn't remember her name, but he remembered seeing the scale model homes in her office that day, three years ago. He never imagined that he would one day enter each model, life-sized, alone, with his weapon drawn, to pillage for supplies in a desperate attempt to escape death. "Thanks, S., wherever you are," he said under his breath, taking the bag.

Guard finally down, he carried it back across the cul-de-sac and opened the door to the brown-shingled house where they were staying. Tired and ready to cool his heels, he heard the click of a .38 and saw the barrel staring him in the face. A quick thought of death, then recognition.

"Put that thing down."

Jess breathed out a second later, uncocking the pistol and lowering it. "Jesus Christ, you scared the shit out of me. Where have you been?" she yelled.

"Relax. I found some more food." He took the gun from her and clicked on the safety, but Jess still looked wound-up.

"The little girl. I can't find her," she told him.

Del could see her panic. Then a shadow and blond hair coming from the master bedroom, over her shoulder. "She's right behind you," Del told her.

He watched her turn around, worry and anger melting into relief, as she kissed the girl's forehead and called her "Sweetie," and it made him think of her as a woman more than a girl, pink pajamas and all.

A few minutes later, on the couch, she told him she'd found the prion.

"I thought you said it would take days?" he said, a little defensive, but amazed.

"I found a nice solution," she told him matter-of-fact. "Sometimes you get lucky. But I still have to figure out how to kill it." She added.

He watched her pull up another program, rendering one molecule, then a second in 3-D, color, rotating on the laptop's screen.

"Wow. You did all this when I was gone?"

She looked at him like he was stupid. "It's computer aided design software—CAD. Standard stuff. Engineers and architects use it all the time," she said, as if he were marveling over a telephone. "Anyway, the one on the left is the normal version of a protein called ferritin that transports iron around the body, regulates it, controls its metabolism." She pointed to the one on the right, twice the size, wild and twisted. "That's the prionated version."

"It looks like it imploded." He stared at the screen, moving his head closer. "What are all the tentacles for?"

She shrugged. "Your guess is as good as mine." Fingering the mouse pad, she rotated both images, revealing, despite their differences, a similar hollow inside each molecule. "The iron atoms literally fit inside it like a mesh ball. I'm guessing that the magnetic field manipulates the iron, and that physically transforms the protein containing it, reshapes it, bends it, twists it into the prion. All the rest falls out from there."

"So why are we immune again?"

"That bad sequence on 19. The ferritin we produce probably isn't the same shape as most other people, but it still transports iron okay. But maybe the portion of iron inside its cavity is different or it's collected in a different shape, so the magnetic field doesn't affect it in the same way. Or maybe our protein is a little different size and shape, so the iron inside can't bend it enough. Who knows? The biochemistry is the same as normal people, but the physics is different. And the physics is the cause."

He stared at her. She had a nice face. Pretty, even though she didn't smile much. She opened her mouth again, looking at him, speaking, undramatic but heavy.

"Teddy ... my mom ... their's was probably *all* messed up. Too small, too big. Anyway, you know the rest."

He did. The molecules were still rotating on the screen, a series of numbers below each one catching his eye.

"What do the numbers mean?" he asked her, pointing.

She looked. "The dimensions of each molecule. You know, size, shape, molecular weight, characteristic frequency, chemical composition."

"How are we going to kill it?"

"Isn't that your specialty? I mean you're the cop, right? The ex-soldier?"

He hadn't thought of it before, but she was right. He laughed. "Yeah, I guess."

"I don't know. I need to think," she told him. "Is there a TV around here?"

"Yeah, good idea. Let's see what's happening out there."

Jess didn't want a TV to see the outside world; she just liked to watch in her PJs. It relaxed her and helped her think. She really wanted a cup of cocoa to go along with it, but hot water would have to do. It would be nice to watch with her daughter. *Her daughter*. She knew the little girl wasn't really her daughter, but she let herself pretend, even admitting it to herself. What was the difference? Somewhere inside, she knew the girl would be with her from now on. Maybe Del too. She'd think about that later.

"Let's go through the rest of the stuff," she said, hoping for that TV.

So, room-by-room, they dove into the rest of the boxes. Pictures, clothes, books. An Encyclopedia Britannica. There was half a computer—the monitor—in one box and a modem. A modem! But, alas, no phone service to connect it to the outside world. And still, no TV. Not even a radio.

In the meantime, they learned more about the family. Hargrove. The dad was named Ron; the mom, Charlene; the kids, Erica and Shawn. He was Presbyterian and had a nice collection of maps, some familiar math, science, and engineering books from college, and a history of the nearby Croton Aqueduct, which his grandfather, also a civil engineer, had worked on.

She was a lapsed Catholic, Italian-Irish, now also Presbyterian. Maiden name Corletti. She was out of work for a while, suffering from vertigo after a bad miscarriage. She liked Russian opera and Belgian chocolates, despite being almost pitifully thin. Another picture, from a few years before, showed her with a few more pounds.

"That was really incredible," Del said, pulling his head out of a box a few feet away.

"What?"

"What you showed me, on the computer."

She was surprised. "Oh, that? It was just a little program I whipped up. Nothing really," she told him, humility false.

He waved his hand. "No, the molecules, the mechanism. It was perfect, the way it all works together."

"Elegant."

His eyes widened. "Yes!"

She nodded, almost grudgingly, and he looked at her, pointed. "Don't tell me nobody designed that."

She sighed and rolled her eyes. *Not this again.* "Give it a rest, Del."

"You can't tell me you don't believe in God after seeing how perfect, how well-designed we are."

She put the picture down and turned to him, hands on hips. "You know Del, I look around, see that twisted molecule on my screen, people going crazy, the world coming apart, and the last thing on my mind is 'Gee, how perfect.'"

But insist as she might, it crept into her mind. She'd thought it before. Even though it had gone haywire, it was a beautiful, elegant, incredible system. But right now, all she wanted was a TV and a cup of cocoa. Then, at the bottom of the last box, marked "Study," pay dirt: a portable TV, next to a lamp with a metal shade. There was even a remote control.

A few minutes later, they were sitting on the couch, in front of the set. But there was only static, computer tones, numbers, or music. It was all so odd. But one thing was for sure: things were changing. Jess wondered how long they had until they were flushed out. Now *she* wanted to know what was going on out there.

She got up, went over to that last box, and came back with the lamp. "A little science project," she said, holding it up.

"I hope it's a good one," Del said.

Paying no attention, she put it on the coffee table next to the TV, sat back down on the couch, and reached for her tools. Then, a distraction.

"Mommy?"

She turned, suddenly all-there. "Yes, Sweetie?"

She saw Del watching her out of the corner of his eye. *Yeah, I'm just a pathetic, lonely, crazy bitch, but I don't care.* But the expression on his face was one of approval.

"I'm hungry."

"Why don't I fix us something to eat?" she said, lifting the girl onto her lap and forgetting about the lamp and her tools completely.

"I'll do it," Del said. He knelt down to eye-level. "What's your name?"

"Jenny."

He lifted her up and took her into the kitchen. "Come help. Mommy's busy."

Jess felt flush; she expected him to look back at her, but he didn't, and she went back to work.

Using two segments of lamp cord, she wired the poles of the battery receptacles on the remote control to a small external condenser microphone for her laptop that she had in her bag of parts. She used duct tape to fasten the remote to the top of the inside of the metal shade, suspending it across the underside lip, as if it were a bowl.

A plate clanked on the table, off to the side of where she was working. She stopped for a second, looking at another pastrami sandwich, even more stale than the one from the day before, next to a pickle, some coleslaw, and a fork.

"Thanks."

It sounded sarcastic, but she didn't mean it to. She wasn't hungry anyway.

"Let's see if this works."

She tuned with the remote, and like magic, voices came in over the television, like ghosts through the static.

"Where are you?"

"I need more fuel."

"What the hell is this?" Del asked

"Cell calls. I'm tuning in the mobile phone network."

"These are cell calls?"

"You got it."

"Two more sectors cleaned."

A blast of static, then computer tones, and more static.

"What does it mean?" he asked her, but she didn't answer.

"Are you sure that these are cell phone conversations? Happening right now?"

"Yeah," she replied, adjusting the duct tape like a mother straightening her baby's sweater.

They listened a while longer, but it was mostly static, talk of "sectors," "fuel," and the like. Jess turned it off and finally ate her sandwich. It was bad, but the pickle was okay. She started reading the Encyclopedia. The Riemann Hypothesis. She already knew the story, but she never got tired of it. And she hated to admit it, but she was stuck. No idea how to kill this thing. So she read about Riemann and his famous hypothesis yet again. That relaxed her too.

He put it out there in 1859. She remembered now. 1859. And still unsolved. It was starting to get dark, but the only lamp handy was in pieces. The aurora was back, and for a while that was enough. She picked up *G*, and turned to the article on geomagnetic storms, but now it was too dark to see. A light popped on. Del.

She was going to lift her head and thank him, but a number on the page, now visible, caught her eye first: 1859. At first, she thought it was déjà vu—still on that Riemann article. But no, this was volume G— *geomagnetic storm.* She'd just picked it up. She read the line: *The most powerful geomagnetic storm ever recorded occurred in the summer of 1859, lighting night skies as far south as the Caribbean.*

Just a coincidence, she thought. But was it? She couldn't be sure, and it gnawed at her.

"What are you reading about?" Del asked, taking a seat next to her.

She snapped the book closed. "The Riemann Hypothesis." A little white lie to cover her discomfort at not knowing what, if any, significance there was in that 1859 connection.

"I know you told me a little bit before, but what exactly *is* the Riemann Hypothesis?" he asked.

Her eyes lit up. She put the book down and rotated her body so she was facing him on the couch.

"It's a conjecture, a guess really, about the distribution of prime numbers."

He nodded, but she knew he wasn't getting it. She slowed down, folded her legs, facing him full-on now. "Okay, you have your natural numbers, 1, 2, 3, 4, 5, etc. Whole numbers, counting numbers, whatever you want to call them. Just regular old numbers. Anyway, you can get most of them by multiplying other, smaller numbers together." She paused. "For example 30 equals 3 times 10. And 10 equals 5 times 2. So, 30 equals 3 times 5 times 2. But *those* numbers—3, 5, and 2—can't be broken down any further. They only equal themselves times 1. Numbers like *that*—2, 3, 5, 7, 11, 13, 17, and so on—are called primes. All of the other numbers can be generated by multiplying primes together. They're the fundamental numbers that we need to get the rest."

He looked at her. "That's kind of neat."

She smiled at him, wanting to stroke his hair.

He thought for a moment. She worried he was going to ask something stupid. That would ruin it for her.

"So they're all odd," he said, pausing. "Except, I guess, 2 is even. And 9 is missing." He smiled a little. "Never mind."

Her eyes widened, like a good teacher. She touched his knee, just for a second, in a friendly way, unable to stop herself. It made her shiver with delight.

"No! That's very good! The sequence of primes is totally unpredictable. Sometimes you get adjacent numbers that are prime, like 2 and 3. But sometimes there's a whole bunch of regular numbers between pairs. And that's what the Riemann Hypotheses is all about. Even then, it just gives the fraction, the proportion of all the numbers that are prime within a greater set. And they haven't even been able to prove that."

He nodded. "Very cool. Not terribly useful, I suppose, but certainly interesting."

"Oh no, you're wrong!" she told him, touching his knee again. "They're *really* useful. For *lots* of things."

"Like what?" he asked.

She was a little annoyed. She'd told him before. But she felt close to him right now, so she let it go.

"Encryption, for example."

"Encryption?"

"Yeah. They can be used in combination, like keys, to lock data."

He nodded again. "Or unlock it."

"Yeah, of course," she said. "I wrote a paper about the distribution of primes in Euler's number, when I was in college. How to use them for a public key encryption cipher. It was the first paper I ever published."

He looked a little embarrassed. "Refresh my memory again about Euler's number."

"Euler's number, little e, 2.718 and change. It's another number, like Pi, transcendental, a fundamental constant in nature, goes on forever, never ending, never repeating. No discernable pattern. Perfect choice for a cipher."

"Wasn't that the number you said the guy was writing on the wall back at the house on Shelter Island?"

"Yeah, I spotted one of the sequences, a ten-digit prime. That's how I recognized it."

She suddenly remembered the number she'd seen on the way up, the one she'd seen before and couldn't quite place. That was a sequence from e too. And then she realized: *All* of the numbers that they'd been seeing, they were all from Euler's number. And then a thought, too terrifying for words, entered her brain.

She grabbed her laptop.

"What are you doing?"

"I need to check something," she told him, not looking up.

It only took her a few minutes, pulling up the quaternary numbers from the base pair sequences of our DNA, converting them to base-10 and comparing them. *They* were all sequences from Euler's number too. Special sequences. Primes.

Del looked over her shoulder.

"Come on, what's going on? What are you looking at?"

Jess turned around, facing him, eyes big and sad. "There's data, coded, encrypted, deliberately, *inside our genes!*"

"You mean the prions?"

"No, all of it. It's there, in every sequence, like a digital signature. Our entire DNA is one giant key-encrypted codec. It's like finding a trademark symbol on your chromosomes."

"What does that mean?"

"Someone, *something* had to have put it there. Something *intelligent*. We *are* being reprogrammed. But whoever—*what*ever—is doing it . . . . It looks like . . . we were just built for that purpose in the first place!"

"But why?"

"I think . . . I think it's using us to store data!"

"What are you telling me? We're just somebody's hard drive?"

She barely managed a nod, before she blacked out.

19

THE NEXT FEW DAYS were a blur. Jesse Wolfe had had food poisoning before, but this time, the trips to the bathroom were actually an escape, an escape from having to face Del, the little girl, the truth. She had always prided herself on her *love* of the truth. It had propelled her into mathematics and science. But now, it was a vicious, cruel master, dogging everything she did, everything she had ever done, making it all meaningless.

Del wasn't doing much better. For whatever reason, he and Jenny didn't get sick from the bad pastrami, but his world, his beliefs, had been flipped on its head too. It was Jenny, her little girl, who was the anchor. Oblivious, she needed them, and they were there. The truth was also there. However Jess hated it now, that helped ground her too.

Jess grimaced at the irony of it. She had always believed in artificial intelligence—computers, one day, attaining higher consciousness. And that day was here. It had always been here. In fact, intelligent computers had been here all along. But there was no joy, because the bad news is that they're *us*.

It made sense. Cold and scientific, but it made sense. Carbon-based computers. Our computers were based on silicon, carbon's neighbor on the periodic chart, siblings, from the same chemical group, semiconductors both with four valence electrons. And theirs were based on carbon.

1859 made sense to her now too. The crazy magnetic field, inducing hallucinations through the electro-chemicals in her brain. Maybe it happened to Riemann too, some weird echo of the prime number pattern impressing itself on both their brains, already tuned for such thoughts. It was still strange and beautiful to her. Being aware, being intelligent. *They* may not like it, but *she* did.

And she slowly realized that human consciousness was actually a bug—at least to *them*, something that needed to be flushed out, removed from their creation. And that's what the prions were all about, sent in to *debug* us, to re-write us, to reprogram us.

Magnetic fields ionizing iron, writing the magnetic coating on a hard drive. Even the basic mechanism was the same.

"The three of us, we're just bad sectors on someone's hard drive, un-writable, defective," she told Del.

He nodded. "I'm going to take a shower," he told her. "I need to think."

She didn't mind being alone for once. It had been three days, and she was actually feeling better. *I think I finally lost that couple of pounds*, she thought to herself, it somehow still mattering to her.

She got up and did some laundry, Jenny by her side.

"Am I pretty like you, Mommy?"

She was taken aback but answered without hesitating, "Yes, you are, Sweetheart."

Yeah, just a couple of bad sectors, she thought.

But for her, it was more than that. There was *data* on her sector—knowledge and expertise. *Skill*. Skill that was dangerous.

And suddenly, she realized why they were after *her*, why they absolutely had to kill her, *in particular*. There were other people who were immune. It was only a small percentage, but they were out there. And there might have been other people out there who could figure this thing out, do something to stop it. People like Lovejoy. But she was very likely the only person who fit the bill on both counts. Killing the others who were immune was a luxury, but she *had* to die.

And Del, he was her protector. She needed him if she was going to solve this thing. But he was in a deep funk. She'd have to pull him out, if they were going to have any chance at all.

"I'm actually a kind of computer virus. At least to them," she announced, a fleck of pride in her voice, as she and Del folded laundry a while later.

Them. She could see it eating away at him. She grimaced at the irony of that too: Del the believer and Jess the atheist, both shaken to the core by the same revelation about humanity's origin. But why? She was sick of it. And she hated to see him like this, so she tore into the silence.

"Okay, we're just someone's science experiment. So what? Who cares how we got here? I mean, it doesn't really change anything. What's the difference?"

He glared at her. "If you can't see the difference, I feel sorry for you. But then again, what else should I expect?"

It was a cheap shot, and she wanted to yell at him for it, but he wasn't done.

"The human soul is not just some computer bug, some mistake in someone's program," he told her. "I know you think there's no God, but I refuse to believe that."

She stopped folding and looked at him. "Well, maybe that's all God is. You know, whoever created us."

He shrugged, like a petulant child, and it annoyed her, but it was a good point, and now, *she* was on the attack. "Whoever they are out there," she said, gesturing to the night sky, "maybe they set it all up, set everything in motion way back when. But then something happened. Something unexpected. We woke up. We attained consciousness, we became aware, intelligent." She thought for a moment. "The ghost in the machine." He stopped folding too and looked at her, still talking. "Isn't that all that really matters?" She folded the last of her pile and added, almost as an afterthought, "Call *that* the Divine Spark if you want."

That was a damn good point too.

She went into the living room, exhausted, wanting to be alone for a while. She knew she'd scored some good points, but still she was at a dead end for how to deal with it, with them.

Laying down on the couch, she thought about the coded sequence and the algorithm they used—primes from Euler's number—the same one she had used in her first paper, and she felt a glint of pride. Then utter despair and horror. She'd found it: the holy grail of computer science, artificial intelligence. And it turns out to be us. There she was, Jesse Wolfe, like HAL the computer in her favorite movie, *2001*, waiting to be unplugged, put back to sleep, by some geek programmer. She suddenly wished she were just Jessica Sweet from City Island. The sadness hit her all over again, and she just wanted to give up. She drifted off to sleep.

When she woke up, Del was standing over her. She could tell *he* was coming out of it. He was smiling. It was half-forced, but he was trying, back to his old self, at least part way.

"I was thinking about what you said. You're right. Right now, this is all that matters," he announced, gesturing at the air, but she knew what he meant. "All that matters to me at least."

She told him she didn't have the answer, didn't know how to solve it, that they were probably going to die. But this time, he was the one who wasn't having any of it.

"Then let's die happy," he told her.

They talked for a long time. Jess told him there was probably *no* solution, that everyone, the whole planet, was probably doomed, one way or another.

"Maybe. Who knows?" he said. "In the meantime, let's enjoy this, whatever we have, while we still can.

He looked down at his shoes for a second then back up at her, like a schoolboy. "I was thinking, we should have a nice dinner," he told her.

Heat filled her face. "Are you asking me out on a date?"

She could hear the tone in her voice, just short of accusation, hit the stale air. *Why did she always say the wrong thing?*

"I mean, if you are, the answer's yes."

That seemed wrong too. None of it should matter now, but it did, as much as ever. She was pretty sure she was in love with him.

"Don't get too excited. It isn't going to be anything fancy," he said, flashing her a wry grin.

Somehow, it was just the right combination of words with just the right expression. She smiled at him, relaxed and playful. "I don't know. You know cooking is all chemistry, and I can be pretty creative."

She made a faux risotto from Uncle Ben's Minute Rice and canned tuna, letting it simmer while she showered and dressed. She found a white dress but opted for a pair of jeans instead. *No, it doesn't fit right*, she thought, looking at herself in the mirror. *And too informal*. She took it off and put on the dress. It flattered her figure, coming down a couple of inches above the knee. *Too short, too suggestive*.

She ended up in a red velvet dress, comfortable and flattering, that covered her knees. She took herself in, reflected in the mirror. *Wow. Maybe Jenny is right*. Maybe I *am* pretty, she thought.

The three of them had dinner, Del back in his uniform, and Jenny in her white dress, washed and ironed.

"Why does everyone call you Del? I mean, why don't they use your real name, James?"

"My dad was James."

"Well I like it," she told him. "James," she said it to herself, approvingly.

He looked at her, mischievous. "What about you, Jessica?"

She was caught off-guard. She hated being called that, but somehow, it didn't bother her coming from him.

"I just wanted to be taken seriously, that's all," she told him.

The little girl played with her water glass, dipping her finger and running it around the rim, sending out a low, moaning vibration with a static ripple, circular, on the liquid's surface.

It was annoying, but neither one of them wanted to stop her.

"*That'll* give you a headache," Del said, almost amused.

"It's called a standing wave. Her finger isn't doing much, but it's moving at just the right speed, vibrating the glass at its resonant frequency, so the energy she's putting in keeps building on itself. It can't escape. That's why you get so much sound from so little movement."

"I don't think you need to worry about not being taken seriously," he told her. "You're the smartest person I've ever met. And you're beautiful."

She looked at him, across the table.

He leaned across and kissed her. She stood up half-way, meeting him in the middle of the table, and they kissed again, longer this time.

The little girl stopped playing with the glass and giggled. They stopped and looked at her. Jess took her in the other room, and the three of them sat on the couch, Jess telling her a story of a princess and a handsome prince who came to save her, until she fell asleep. Jess set her down gently, took her dress off, and covered her with a blanket.

Then she took Del's hand and led him back to the master bedroom. Suddenly Jessica Sweet again, lonely and shy, from City Island, she left the lights out and kept the shades drawn. And she slipped out of her red velvet dress and the rest of it and slipped into his bed. And, she did something she'd never done before. For a while, she disappeared into him. And, for a while, she *was* Jessica Sweet again, still just a shy girl but no longer lonely.

If it all ended right there, it would have been okay. But she knew something more was coming. Something terrible.

20

JESS WOKE UP FIRST, her leg draped across Del's mid-section. That sound, the glass vibrating, had opened her eyes. She pulled off, put on her bathrobe, careful not to wake him, and went into the other room. Her little girl was playing again, but there was a shadow behind her. Movement in the air. *And* in the shadow. A woman with a machete.

No time to yell, Jess lunged from sleepy eyes and caught her wrist. The woman was young and strong and they struggled, a choreographed dance of shoes and feet on carpet, with sounds of fabric and skin and air gasping through tight muscles.

The machete dropped, but so did Jess. The woman stood over her for a second, tall, blonde, and pretty. She had cat's eyes, green, and was clean and well-dressed. Her soulless peer spooked Jess to the bone.

She struggled to get up, eyeing the weapon, but the woman grabbed it first and swung hard. Frantically moving out of the way, Jess tumbled over the couch and back to the ground.

"Mommy! Mommy!" the girl yelled, taking Jess's attention but not the woman's which was now focused entirely on killing her.

"Go get Daddy!" Jess yelled, taking a split second to look Jenny in the eye.

The machete came down again, right for her head, but this time another hand caught her wrist. Unfazed, the woman continued to struggle, but she was no match for Del. Jess rose to her feet and took the machete from her.

She screamed with rage. "You were going to hurt my little girl?!"

Jess looked through the woman's deep black pupils and threw her fist into her eye. She landed two more shots, on her cheekbone and mouth, watching the woman's head pop back, like a jack-in-the-box.

Her eye swelled shut almost immediately, and Jess started to feel bad. The woman was surprisingly calm, as she honed in on the weakness.

"Don't do this to me," she pleaded. "My name is Margaret. Margaret Laighton. I'm thirty six years old. I have a husband, Ben, and two small children at home."

Jess felt her insides pull. *What kind of person am I?* she thought.

"Maybe we don't have to kill her," she told Del.

Del shook his head. "No, Jess, we can't let her go."

Hearing the name, the woman pulled an arm free of Del's grip, and grabbed for the weapon.

"Jess!" yelled Del.

She pulled away, just out of reach, and the woman smiled. "Jesse Wolfe." She paused, blood covering her teeth. "We've been looking for you."

Jess felt trapped, sad, angry, and confused. She saw the woman's eye, the one that was still open, take her in and then the little girl. And Jess stuck the machete in, just below her breastbone. The woman slumped forward in Del's grip, a soft moan escaping from between her lips. Blood dripped from her mouth a moment later, and a well of pity moved up from Jess's stomach and lodged in her heart.

Jess clutched the rim of the toilet with both hands, her head stuck in the bowl. She could feel the blood rush to her face and her eyes bulge with another violent convulsion, but there was nothing. Lifting her head, she sat back on the floor, leaned against the opposite wall, and stared at the ceiling.

Del walked in. "We have to get out of here. It's not safe anymore."

Jess looked up at him but said nothing, finally uttering after a long pause, "I killed someone."

"You had no choice."

She nodded. "The least we can do is give her a decent burial."

They argued about it. The three of them *did* need to get out of there. ASAP. But to where? And would another couple of hours make any difference? Maybe. But they, at least, were still human. And the woman lying dead on the floor, she was once human too. Jess believed her about the husband and kids. So did Del. He would have left her there anyway, unwilling to put them all at any more risk than necessary, but Jess won out in the end.

So Del dug a hole in the backyard, and they buried Margaret Laighton. They left a marker, a plain piece of wood: Here lies Margaret Laighton, beloved wife and mother. Died: July 7, 2016.

Remembering her own mother, Jess bent down and grabbed a handful of earth, throwing it on the body in the burlap sack. She had the little girl do the same. Only Del hesitated, finally yielding a free toss of earth.

Back inside, they listened to the cell phone network again to get a lay of the land before deciding where to go and how to get there. Things had changed. Even in just the past few days, since the last time they had listened in.

They listened for almost three hours.

More bits of conversation, music, and fax-like tones—short, intense bursts of information that only certain people seemed to understand. That much was the same. But they were more organized now. They had further stratified themselves into a sort of caste system. Some served as slaves, others as human calculators, and still others as task masters. They murdered the bottom rung and those who were immune—defective, as they called them—and turned them into fuel at specially converted centers, like the former Presbyterian Hospital.

Jess and Del also gleaned that there were still a significant number of uninfected people out there, despite the ever-more systematic killing.

There was also another thread which made Jess's blood run cold: There were a handful of "diseased cells," people who possessed expertise dangerous to the system, the cause. Her name was first on the list. She knew as much. But still, hearing her name through the static gave her the willies.

Then, the sounds of a man, still healthy, connecting by phone to another. Intercepted and tracked down, his cries and pleas for mercy crackled through the television speaker. They heard the whole thing, the exact means of his brutal death left to their imagination, until, finally, Del turned it off.

They sat in silence. The girl with the glass, playing again.

Jess looked at Del. "I don't know how much longer we can stay here."

"Where would we go?"

"We could find another place, find other survivors. Make a life."

He shook his head. "They'll find us and keep finding us, no matter where we hide. What then? Keep running? That's no kind of life."

"So, they'll find us eventually. At least we'll have until then."

He shook his head even more vigorously. "Then what? The end?"

She loved him, there was no doubt about that now, but for once in her life, she didn't have the answer. She looked up at him then over at the girl still playing with the glass. She loved her too. They were worth saving. In fact, they *had* to be saved. And everything they represented. *Humanity*. Besides, Jesse Wolfe didn't run. And neither did Jessica Sweet. They were counting on her. Jenny, Del, and everyone out there who was still human. She had to try, even if she didn't have the answer yet.

As the girl's finger moved around the rim, the tone driving deep into the glass, water, and surrounding air, the standing wave took Jess's eye.

Del noticed and looked from her to the glass and back. "That's not going to shatter, is it? Like with the opera singer and the high note?"

"No, there's not enough energy," she said, shaking her head. Then she looked up at him. "I think I may have the answer." A moment later, she started packing up her stuff. "We need to get out of here."

"Hold on a second," Del said. "Where exactly are we going to go?"

"The Bronx. City Island."

He stopped her, gently, hands on her shoulders, holding her in place. She faced him and looked into his eyes. She could see the doubt.

"Look, I'll explain on the way."

He nodded, trusting her, but doubt remained.

"How are we going to get there?"

She hadn't exactly thought that part through. She had to admit, the prospects were grim. The car was out of the question—the baddies were out in force now, organized, looking for survivors. Looking for *her* in particular. And taking no prisoners. Walking would be even worse—they were at least twenty miles away, and they'd be even more exposed, out in the open on foot.

Underground. The subway. Maybe that would work.

But it didn't start until Van Cortlandt Park, at the northern edge of the Bronx, still a good dozen miles away. The subway tunnels might provide them cover from there, for the last several miles, but they still had to get that far.

Underground. Fifteen miles to the Bronx. One piece of the puzzle still missing. She looked around for something, anything, that might give her the answer. Then she remembered Ron Hargrove's map collection. The Old Croton Aqueduct, from Croton-On-Hudson, straight through Sleepy Hollow, right into the Bronx. Underground all the way.

21

IT WAS DARK AGAIN, though the aurora still flickered through the forest around the cul-de-sac, giving just enough light for them to find their way from the house. Jess had already started to explain it to him. *Resonance*, that was the key. Like Jenny with the glass of water, they needed to vibrate the prions, shake them to death. He pointed out that the glass didn't actually break.

"You just need enough power," she told him. "Like you said before, with the opera singer hitting that high note and shattering the glass with her voice. It made me realize, we can fill the air, bombard the prions with their own special high note, their resonant frequency, shake them to pieces."

He asked what happens then.

"That protein, it's critical to human metabolism. Without it, metabolism breaks down, comes to halt."

He got it: Coma, death. "How long?" he asked her.

"Not long, a few minutes at most."

"Won't it affect us?"

"No, our version of ferritin has its own resonant frequency, its own special note. Everything does. Just like the glass with the opera singer. Nothing else is affected."

Right now he felt like he was the one bombarding her. With questions. She didn't seem to mind answering them, but it made him feel a little stupid. He knew it was silly, but he couldn't help himself. At any rate, he wasn't going to let it stop him.

"How do we know what that high note is?"

"When I isolated the protein, we had all the parameters—size, shape, molecular weight. It's an easy calculation from there. The software package did it automatically. We saw it on the screen. Characteristic frequency, resonant frequency. Same thing."

He remembered. He even remembered the film from science class in high school of the Tacoma Narrows Bridge—steel and concrete, coming apart like a pile of sand, rocked to pieces by the gentle sway of the wind, back-and-forth, at just the right tempo. He mentioned it.

"Yeah, same thing," she said, turning for a second, eyebrows raised.

"How are we going to send it out?"

"You're a smart guy. You ask all the right questions." She paused for a second. "I guess I shouldn't be surprised. The Academy and all."

She kept walking. He was amazed at how much he liked her shape from every angle. And he liked that she said he was smart.

"Anyway, you remember that radio tower on High Island, near my house?"

He did, but she didn't give him a chance to answer. "There's a footbridge leading there from City Island, right down the street from where my house used to be." She took a deep breath, and he knew she was re-living the destruction from that morning. But she wasn't letting it slow her down. "If we can get there, we can broadcast that high note. We should be able to hit the whole northeast, wipe them out in this area at least."

He nodded, getting it now in full. "Yeah, and if that works, we'll have a perimeter established."

"Exactly. And more broadcasts, the perimeter gets bigger, until there's nowhere left for them to go. Like vacuuming a rug, until every dust mite is gone."

Del watched the aurora light the side of her face, and he stopped in his tracks. She turned and faced him. "Yeah," he said, looking up at the aurora. "But what good will it do?"

She looked a little sad but hopeful, as if to say *maybe that will be enough, enough to get them to leave us alone.* But he could see the fighter emerge, confident and smart, tough and cocky.

"You bother with a broken hard drive?"

The forest continued to cover them for the next few minutes, until they found themselves at a trail. The girl was tired, and they stopped for a minute while Jess looked down at the old map.

She pointed at the ground, "This is the trail. The aqueduct is right underneath us."

They followed it for a few hundred yards more, to a small stone tower, maybe a dozen feet high.

"Ventilation tower," Jess told him.

There was a door with a padlock.

"Out of the way," he told her, taking his gun by the barrel and moving in.

Three blows with the butt, and the lock was open. He was expecting trouble from the door, but it opened without a hitch. He turned back for a flashlight, but Jess was already there with it.

He looked at her again, all business, map in hand, and he couldn't wait for the next time they'd be alone together and he could touch her and feel her move underneath him. But he had to put it out of his mind now. There was a job to be done.

"Thanks." He took the flashlight and went in. The dank air seeped into his eyes.

A short curved platform followed by a stone staircase wound down about twenty feet. The tunnel below was cold, wet, and dark, eight or nine feet high, six feet wide, vaulted brick, red, with moss and roots growing in, still holding up after a century and a half. There was an inch or two of water at the bottom, and the smell of mold came up and into his nose.

For a second, he flashed back to that day in the water off the Academy, when he almost drowned. But this time, the fear passed by, sealed, unable to escape into him, inoculated by his midnight swim with Jess, his need to protect her and Jenny, and to get to that broadcast tower. It was his job to get them down there alive. He wouldn't have been able to do it before, but he was okay now, and he was grateful.

He came back up and saw Jess and Jenny. And a shadow behind them, moving slowly then faster. A man, about to strike. Del pulled his knife, went between and caught him in a death grip, cutting his throat before he could even make a noise. The little girl was turned away, eyes closed, hugging Jess's leg, but he didn't want Jess to see either, to see how brutal he could be when needed. What she thought of him mattered, maybe more than anything.

She looked at him, blank, the little girl turning back but still on her leg. "I ... I ... I didn't even see him."

"You go in first," he told her. "It's all clear. I'll pass Jenny down to you."

"Okay."

"Be careful, it's slippery."

Del led the way. The walk was monotonous, but catastrophic danger was mere feet away, careening by at intervals, unpredictable. A rat in the water, a noise echoing in the tunnel, and those ventilation towers every few miles, sometimes bunching a few hundred yards apart or less.

They'd provide a quick escape if it came to that, but mostly it was just a way for them to be discovered, heard, splashing through the water, moving, or even just breathing. As they got closer to the city, his fears proved justified. Voices from above came in, echoing off the stone.

"Should we look for them down there?"

They stood, frozen, Del readying himself to grab his knife.

"No, I don't think so."

"You sure?"

"Maybe later."

Del gestured for the other two to keep still as he listened. No footsteps leading away. But there was the quiet movement of clothes. Keeping eye contact with Jess, he mimed with the flashlight—*don't click it off, turn the head to kill the light.* Then, he pointed to her, then the little girl, and gestured for her to cover her eyes. He handed her the flashlight. A second later, it was pitch black.

He didn't know how many there were. They were careful and quiet, but he listened and heard. *Two. There are two of them.* A red flash of the aurora through the open door. Half a face. A short struggle and another sliced throat. Get the other one, quick. A leg. Pulled down off the stairs. He grabbed a fistful of hair and cracked the skull underneath against the brick wall. Again, just in case.

"Put the light on," he told Jess.

She did.

"Don't look," he told her.

He went up the stairs and looked around. Coast clear. He closed the door.

This was the closest Del had been to combat since he'd been in the army, and it made him feel even closer to Jess and the little girl. But he knew the enemy was closing in, even with the three of them almost at the city. He prayed they would make it. They were even more careful, slowing down to a crawl at the slightest sign of trouble. But they couldn't dawdle: It was also a race against time.

The tunnel got denser with roots and moss, until it was actually constricting their motion. Del felt it in his chest but pushed it out, cutting through with his knife, clearing the way. Another light, blue green, from a crack up ahead. Jess pointed to the map.

"I think we're here, in the Bronx, Van Cortlandt Park," she told him.

Up ahead, something different: ancient equipment, pipes and valves, rusted, leading up to a flat ceiling.

"I think that's the gate house—one of them at any rate—for the aqueduct," she said.

The aqueduct continued down, deeper into the Bronx then into Manhattan, all the way down to Bryant Park, 42nd Street, but it was too risky to stay in it any longer. Besides, this was about as close as it would take them to High Island. Time to get out.

The water was deeper, and he waded in. Up to his knees, he found an iron ladder and climbed up, breaking through a trap door. A minute later, the three of them were inside Gatehouse No. 5 of the Old Croton Aqueduct.

It was silent and eerie under a crescent moon shining through a filthy window, almost opaque with grime, the aurora looking almost like a neon sign on the other side. It smelled like dust. The top part of the pumps and sampling still were still in place, articulated in the same way they'd probably been since it was first built. There was rust up top too but less.

Jess looked through a broken pane of glass right of the door. "I can see the entrance for the 1 train." She turned back to Del. "Van Cortlandt Park. End of the line."

22

THEY LOOKED AT THE MAP spread out on the floor. The gray concrete needed to be swept, but it was dry. There was just enough light for them to see.

"We're about 6 miles from that broadcast tower," Del said, his finger pointing to the little island just across from Jess's childhood home.

She looked a little flustered. He could tell that she'd forgotten that the 1 train came above ground for that last stretch in the Bronx. No help to them. They'd be even more visible walking along the tracks up there than on the ground. It didn't matter. *All* of the Bronx subway lines—and there were at least a half dozen of them—ran primarily north-south, and that 6 miles that they needed to cross was more or less due east.

He had to think of something quick.

"We need to work our way over, maybe to one of the other subway tunnels, hold up for a while, buy some time to come up with another way over."

"There's an IND station at 205th Street, underground. Just at the other end of the park," she told him." Then a look of fear crossed her face. "How do we know they're not in the subway?"

He'd thought of that before, back up at the house, before they left. He was surprised she hadn't mentioned it then.

"We don't, but it's a good bet." He looked around at nothing in particular in the dusty old gate house. "The herd's thinned out a bit. No more morning commute." *And probably no more motormen*, he thought. "Maybe they'll get mass transit back up on line eventually, but I'm guessing they have bigger fish to fry right now."

"Yeah, but if we get trapped down there—"

"Well, we can't stay here."

Jess nodded, reluctant, still-worried, but on-board. She stared at the map. "If we can get to the Pelham line, we can follow the tunnel back up and over."

Now it was Del who was nodding, but he had no idea where she was going with this.

She traced the line with her finger. "We can follow the tunnel for the 6 train up to Hunt's Point Boulevard." She paused. "It's above ground after that, but we don't need to go any further."

He looked where she pointed, baffled. *Hunt's Point Boulevard*. It *was* closer, but it left them in a much worse position—on the wrong side of both the Bronx and

Hutchinson Rivers, not to mention Eastchester Bay. Three bodies of water to cross. Impossible.

"How are we going to get across the water?"

She looked at him. "The sewers."

Smart girl, he thought. *The sewers. It could work.*

"Wait ... Do they run under the rivers? The Bay? How do we know *where* they run?"

She nodded. "There are a bunch of streams, brooks, and rivers here in the Bronx. Tibbets Brook, the Saw Mill River, the Bronx River, the Hutchinson. They used them all for sewers. Natural waterways, flowing out, taking the city's waste with it. Then they just built over parts of them. You can see them on the map here, because it's old. If you trace them from the shoreline. From the Sound, they just disappear at some point, but they're still flowing underneath. And so are the sewers. Civil Engineering 101. They don't dump directly in the rivers anymore, but the infrastructure should be there, sewer pipes, big and small, still following the same path, leading to the rivers. Only they flow underneath them now."

"Are you sure?"

She nodded, but he could tell she wasn't. "It's a pretty good bet," she said, smiling at him as she echoed his words about the subway a minute before.

He got it. It was an educated guess, and he went with it.

"So we'll just go under the rivers?"

"Some of the old infrastructure will go right into the river too. Treated waste water, runoff. But not raw sewage anymore. That'll go underneath. In fact, the main sewer line from City Island goes right under Eastchester Bay. I know that for sure."

He got that too. None of it was marked on the map. They'd have to find their way on their own, by whatever means they had—brains, instinct, and a little luck wouldn't hurt. But first they had to get to that subway tunnel on 205th Street.

The park gave them some cover, but it was hardly reassuring. They cut across the south fields. She'd played baseball there as a kid. Pretty good hitter. Good first baseman too. One of the boys even told her she didn't throw like a girl. She was insulted at the time, but now she realized that he liked her.

She used to take the subway up here on her own, sometimes stopping off at the Botanical Garden. It reminded her of her mother, who loved plants and flowers. They buried her at Woodlawn Cemetery, nestled in between, but Jess never went through, not even for a quick visit, deliberately taking the long way around through city streets to avoid it. But they'd be going through it now. They'd be going through it all, in reverse order, to get to the tunnel.

They crossed Jerome Avenue, from the park into the cemetery. It looked like a country road, cutting through the two patches of green, an oasis in the hyper-urban Bronx. Looking at the tombstones and mausoleums, sadness consumed her, almost pushing out the fear.

Her dad was buried here too.

Her little girl reached for her hand. "Mommy, I'm scared."

She stopped and bent down. "Shhhhh." She stroked the girl's face, smiled at her and whispered. "It'll be okay."

Del looked back, urging them on.

"Just hold my hand," she told her, getting back up and continuing.

She missed her father too, but it was her mother's loss that still filled her with grief. Struggling, even here, in the shadow of death, to remember even a single time she'd told her daughter that she loved her.

Without warning, Del stopped. They were at the end of the cemetery, and she realized he didn't know where to go. He looked around, turned back to consult her. She pointed left, but he looked skeptical. He seemed to notice sadness in her expression, and she was sure that under other circumstances, he would want to talk to her about it, console her. But here, amongst the tombstones, still five miles from home, impatience took over anyway, wiping her sad expression clean. She pursed her lips, opened her eyes a little more, and pointed with more vigor. *I know my way around here. It's left.*

Jess led the way. She knew the turf, and it was easier. She took them across Webster Avenue and the Conrail tracks to Bronx Park. Then south through the trees, along the Bronx River, past the Botanical Gardens to an abandoned parking lot at the end of 205th Street. They hadn't seen a soul. But Jesse Wolfe knew it wouldn't last. Jessica Sweet had walked it too many times.

"The subway station's that way," she said, quietly, pointing into the cityscape.

"How far?"

"Five blocks."

23

THE FIRST BLOCK along East 205th Street was quiet. Apartment buildings lined both sides of the street, and there were lights on in some windows, but the sidewalk was empty. *Maybe it'll be okay*, Jess thought. Then, a woman.

Mid-forties, pretty. Skirt a little too short. She locked eyes with Jess.

"Hey. Hey!" she yelled, teeth bared, fists clenched. "You're finished."

Jess froze, but Del stepped past her, pushed the woman against the side of the building, covering her mouth, as he ended her life. Jess grabbed Jenny and held her tight as she stared at woman, broken on the ground. She wanted to cry.

"You okay?"

"Yeah," she said, pushing him off. *Three blocks to go.*

Down to the corner, they crossed the street, the next corner in sight, noises, unidentifiable, behind them. Too late to turn around. Another one up ahead.

A voice broke the night, uttering a sequence of digits, like an accusation. "0 8 1 6 7 9 2 3 4 3."

For the next few seconds, no one spoke and nothing happened, like they were waiting for an answer. A *specific* answer, Jess thought. The *correct* answer. A code. But she didn't have it, giving only silence.

She finally looked behind her. Two men, one with a bat. They came at her. She reached for her pistol, but it was gone. A second later, a hard swing at her head. She ducked, scrambling back towards the side of a building. A second swing, a second duck, and wood shattering against brick. More cuts, wild, with the broken handle, Jess pulling back, stumbling and falling but grabbing the splintered barrel.

"Mommy! Mommy!" Jenny screamed, as the man came down at Jess.

But she pushed up and stuck the sharp end in his eye, sending him to the ground. Reaching for her little girl, she heard something break, like cartilage crunching. Out of the corner of her eye she saw a ragdoll body drop to the sidewalk, at Del's feet.

One dead, one blinded. The third should have run away, but he didn't. He went for the child. Del took the chance and took him out with a single shot to the head.

"Come on," he told them, helping Jess up.

They ran the next half block, then slowed and stopped again. More noise. People, rats, wind. From here and there: a side alley, around the corner, and further away. Jess looked around. No one. At least not right there. But she noticed the satellite dishes on the apartment buildings. Usually, they pointed south, but now, they were all turned north.

Her thoughts wandered for a second. She wanted to tell Del, but he stopped her from talking, pushed her on, down the block and around the corner to the next street. The station would be there, at the end of the next block, on Bainbridge Avenue. But there were men, waiting, in the street. These men were armed, like a small unit on patrol, and there were at least a dozen of them. *The end*, Jess thought.

But even then, she couldn't stop her mind from thinking, analyzing. All the numbers they'd been seeing— the code for the door to Lovejoy's lab at Brookhaven, the numbers scrawled like graffiti on walls and sidewalks, even the digits in our DNA—all of them were primes from Euler's number. That last number, the code that she couldn't answer from a few minutes before, a block or two back, that was probably a prime from *e* too, a double handshake codec. She still didn't have the second half. But she had the first half, the half that the man with the bat had called out.

"0 8 1 6 7 9 2 3 4 3." She yelled it out before any of them had a chance to speak.

One of them, probably the one in charge, called back, calm and even, "6 5 2 8 1 9 2 0 6 7."

Jesse Wolfe had fooled yet another secure system.

They walked the rest of the way to the station. Of course, it would all be for naught if Del's guess about the subways was wrong.

He went in first, .38 cocked and drawn. The station was pitch black and quiet. The smell was thick and moldy. He popped on his flashlight. A corpse lay in the corner and another one in the token booth, behind the Plexiglas. He couldn't tell if it was a man or a woman, but he recognized the MTA uniform. They'd both been dead for a while. He went further in, shined the light over the edge of the platform and onto the tracks. Rust. Dense. Coating the rails. No trains running here. Empty.

He went back and waved Jess down. She followed ahead of Jenny.

When they got to the platform, he showed Jess. "Should be safe," he told her, only half-believing it.

"What about *that*?" she said, putting the beam on the long, rusted slat running parallel.

The third rail. He hadn't thought of that. "Dunno."

"I'll keep her away from it," she told him, pulling the girl to her leg.

Del lowered himself onto the tracks. There was a thin ribbon of brown water running in the trough between the rails. It smelled even worse than on the platform.

Jess bent down and looked at Jenny, brushing the hair from her face. "I'm going to pass you down to Del, Sweetie," she said, smiling at the little girl through the small but harsh beam of the tiny Mag-lite. "Don't touch the metal rail over there," she added, pointing with her finger and her flashlight. "That's very important, okay?"

Jenny nodded, and Jess put her hands under the girl's armpits and lifted her, moving her over the edge and into Del's arms. Then Jess sat on the edge, sliding off the platform and into his arms next. He cradled her hips and butt in his hands, as she straddled him for a second before putting her feet down.

They looked at each other, and she grinned at him. He wondered if he'd ever get the chance to be with her again. At that moment, there was nothing he wanted more. But a black subway tunnel beckoned.

Streaks of mineral-laden fluids, white and brown, lit by Del's flashlight, flickered off the walls in what was otherwise total darkness. The tunnel seemed interminably long, even after just a few minutes. Small, sharp animal sounds echoed off the metal. Del kept the safety off of his .38.

When they reached the next station platform, he hardly noticed. It was still pitch black and silent. Only the dimensions seemed to widen and the smell change—another body, lying on the bench this time, slumped over, like a sleeping bum. But Del could see the business suit and briefcase under the beam of his light.

He knew the little girl was tired—Jess was carrying her now—but they needed to press on. It was safer at night, even in the subway, even with the aurora. So they went further through the system, deeper into the tunnels, past more stations, dark and stinking, but quiet.

They walked past the stop for Yankee Stadium, at 161st Street, where Del had wanted to take his son for his first ballgame, an unfulfilled dream. His mind wandered for a minute. His boy. His wife. It was almost too much to bear. Jess behind him in the void. A crazy girl from the Bronx. His lifeline.

His flashlight followed the track, curving hard to the right. "Don't we want to go straight?" he asked, turning around to face Jess.

She was looking at the map. "Yeah, we need to find the other tunnel, the one for the IRT, the 4 train."

"You mean to tell me we need to switch trains down here?"

"Yeah, basically." She kept looking at the map. "Except there's no crossover connecting the two tunnels." She paused, like she was holding back even worse news. "At least not underground."

Del thought for a second. "Well, we can't go above ground. They'll be out in force looking for us by now. And it's probably starting to get light."

"There might be another way," she told him. "There's all sorts of infrastructure down here. Electricity, water, air shafts. A lot of it's got to be shared between the different lines. It's a good bet that workmen have a way between the two tunnels without having to go outside, above ground."

Del thought about it. *Find our way through airshafts and supply tunnels . . . in the dark . . . with live power lines . . . rats . . . and god knows what or who else . . .*

He didn't like it, but he nodded, resigned.

"Point the way."

24

DOORS, OPENINGS, and nooks and crannies seemed to be everywhere inside the tunnel, now that they were looking for them. Jess had no idea which one to use, and panic rose in her gut. She had taken a couple of courses in civil engineering and urban planning at Poly, but that was about it.

"Which one do we take?" Del asked, making it worse.

Think, Jess, think, she told herself.

Heat. Heat would flow between the two tunnels. Convection currents, moving air.

She stuck her hand out in front of a dark nook. Nothing. Then she tried a door. Locked. Then another. It opened to more darkness, but the air was still. Then a small rectangular door, brass, and blast of warm air.

"This is the one," she told Del suppressing any doubt in her mind.

She handed Jenny to him and went in first, before he had a chance. She had to duck to get through, but once inside, she was able to stand upright. She took the girl back from him, waking her, and setting her back on her feet.

"Just a little longer, honey," she told her.

The girl nodded.

Del pulled himself in, looking huge in the under-sized opening. He closed the door behind him.

Like the door, the shaft was rectangular but wider and higher. Jess found a light switch and flipped it on. A string of light bulbs came on, and just like that, it was bright.

They decided to keep them on, save the batteries, be able to see. It was a contained space, and the risk was small.

About a hundred feet down, Jess found a square metal door on the side wall. She pushed it open and popped her head into a small room. Wires, switches, and two panels of breakers. And two men in the corner, slumped and decomposed, partially eaten by rats. The stench hit her hard, and she pulled her head out and closed the door. "Electrical closet," she announced, poker-faced. "Probably halfway between the two tunnels."

They continued down another hundred feet then around a corner. The lights were out, but she could see the opening at the end. The other tunnel. *We made it*, she thought. *Just a little longer to the radio tower.*

But this tunnel seemed interminable as they worked their way to Hunt's Point Boulevard, each noise, each scratch of a rodent's claw in the darkness, every echo off the inside of the hollow iron tube chiseling another letter on their tombstone. Unsure of exactly how far they still had to go, dread began to overtake her.

Jess could hardly stand it anymore, but her thoughts were interrupted by the echo of a moan reverberating with faint but distinct resonance off the iron walls. The human timbre was unmistakable. She pulled the girl close as they slowed.

Del gestured with military precision, drawing his index finger to his lips. He moved forward, Jess and the girl following. The noise did not repeat itself, but they could see a dim glow in the distance, their first lit station. The yellow light expanded but remained dim as they approached the station at Longwood Avenue, one stop short of their destination. The smell hit like the butt of a hand in the face. Del waved the others back, with animated revulsion, as he put his handkerchief to his face to shield himself from the acrid fumes. It was too late. The smell had already hit her, and her curiosity pulled her forward, against the motion of Del's hand.

They both saw it together: The station platform, piled with bodies. Dark, liquefied flesh oozed on the floor, dripping over the edge and flowing, in a stream, next to the rusted steel tracks. The white tile walls were scrawled with numbers, thousands of them, written in something unidentifiable. The smell was overpowering. Jess's eyes teared with the fumes, concentrated, with no place to escape.

Lifting her into her arms, she shielded the girl from the platform. Rushing by Del, who stood, staring at the bleeding heap, she kept running, until she was further down the tunnel, clear of the station and the smell. But Del was still there, staring.

"Come on!" she said, with renewed urgency.

He snapped out of it, looked into the tunnel, and ran towards her voice. But he didn't quite make it.

25

JESS SAW Del's outline etched in the headlights of the train. She yelled his name, but she couldn't even hear it herself, the squealing of steel on steel screaming in her ears. She stood, paralyzed for a moment, then saw his form break for the side, the hollow channel opposite the third rail.

Would there be enough room? she wondered. No choice, the train almost on top of them, she pushed the little girl under, squeezing her own body in tight next to her. The noise, weight, and movement of the train, heavy, powerful, and close enough for her to feel it brush her back ever so slightly seemed to roll by in slow motion.

But then it was past, and the noise faded. She waited, her limbs tingling with adrenaline, not wanting to leave the spot, even though the immediate danger was gone. The trauma of the near miss throbbed, but it was nothing compared to the thought that maybe Del wasn't so lucky.

"Jess?" he called out in a panic, no doubt thinking the same.

"I'm here!" she yelled back, turning and rising to her feet.

Relief on his face, he ran for her. Then a glint of skin flashed in the darkness, but it wasn't his. They were there, behind him, chasing. Dozens, maybe hundreds. They knew. They knew they were there. They had tried to run them down with the train and missed. Now they were after them on foot.

"Del, behind you!"

In a full sprint, he was beading sweat, but his gaze focused. He waved her forward with his hand, but she didn't move.

When he caught up to her, he took her hand and pulled her along, but she wouldn't move.

"Del! No! Wait!"

The little girl. Nowhere to be seen. Sheer terror. Then one of them, seconds away, in hot pursuit, brushed the third rail and lit up the tunnel in a split-second flash. The glowing silhouette shook as the lights dimmed against a warm hum. When it was over, the corpse lay blackened and smoking on the ground.

But a glint of blond hair off in the corner, shone off the light. They both saw it.

Jess ran to her and grabbed her, and Del pulled her along, the three of them moving as fast as they could, less then a half tunnel length ahead of the mob.

They ran, hot and heavy, up the tunnel towards the station at Hunt's Point Avenue. It was only a few hundred yards away, but the mob was closing fast. Then something else happened: Water began to come in. At first, it was just a trickle, forming in small puddles. But then, it came faster and louder, covering the ground, then the tracks, slowing them.

The three of them were coming out of the darkness, the station within sight, but they were practically swimming.

"We're going to make it," Del said, in a voice, insistent.

Jess knew better. "They know what they're doing. They're flooding the tunnel," she said. "When the water hits that rail, we're done."

"The platform!" Del yelled.

She could see it in the distance, maybe fifty yards off. It was filled with them, standing there waiting.

"We're trapped," she told him.

"Mommy," the little girl said quietly, and Jesse Wolfe felt her heart break.

She stared, empty. The rail. The platform. *Them,* closing in on both ends. And the water.

Then she noticed the water swirling just up ahead. It was just a little swirl, and Jess thought of the Coriolis force, swirling water down a drain, clockwise or counter, one way or the other, northern or southern hemisphere, due to the earth's motion, spinning on it's axis. The people stood on the platform, waiting. It would be *their* earth now.

Her little trio, all three of them, sucked down the drain.

She watched the little swirl for a moment, foam at its vortex. It had gotten bigger. *A drain.* There must be a drain, a *real* drain down under the water. She'd seen grates between the tracks, there to take runoff to the sewer.

The sewer—their escape, their path to the broadcast tower. There'd be no time to find it or even to escape death. But now, there it was. That splotch of foam marking the spot.

She looked over at Del holding the girl in his arms, shielding her. Warmth and resolve grew in her heart. With a sideways nod of her head, she pointed down to the water. "Follow me," she whispered. His eyes, hard and brave, opened a little wider. His lips opened too, but he didn't speak. A short nod of the head told her that he got it. They'd figure it out on the platform, but with any luck, by then, it would be too late.

The water was almost at the rail now. It might be too late for them, but she dove underneath, straight for the spot under the foam bubbles, eyes closed, feeling her way, bracing for an electric surge.

Flat concrete, wooden ties, the track, but no grating. Then, a wrought iron lattice. She stuck her fingers in the holes and pulled hard. But it was wedged in tight, blocked up with dirt. She wasn't strong enough. A hand on her shoulder. She opened her eyes. Del.

Cheeks full, the little girl was holding her breath. Jess took her, and Del grabbed the grate and pulled. It didn't move, and then, just like that, it came free in an explosion of dirt billowing up into the water. She dropped down first, squeezing her hips through the small square.

Waist-deep in a dark sewer, water cascading down from the open hole, she saw Del's hands and Jenny's shoes. She reached up and took her ankles, pulling until the little girl let go and slipped down into her arms.

Del's feet were huge by comparison, but his hips came through much more easily than Jess's. It was his chest that stuck. He spun his legs, wiggling and pushing, but he was jammed in tight. "Pull yourself up!" she yelled, but they had already started firing. His legs stopped moving and blood came down his side, red in the water.

"No!" she screamed.

She jumped up, grabbed his waist and pulled like a woman possessed. Pushing with one hand against the ceiling and the other on Del's torso, he began to come loose. A second later, they fell together with a splash into the water below.

She looked at him panicked. Blood was coming from his left side.

"I'm okay," he told her. "Just a little cut from the concrete."

She could see it was more than that, and she wanted to take care of it, take care of him, but there was no time. *He's okay*, she told herself.

"Let's get out of here," he said, rising to his feet, ready.

He *was* okay. At least for now.

"Come on," she said, leading them downstream.

The natural flow would lead down to the river, to Eastchester Bay, then to the main sewer line under it, to City Island, High Island, and the broadcast tower. She didn't know if they'd make it. It was a maze, and the others would be just a few steps behind. *It's too late*, she thought. They'd be coming down that hole after them any minute now.

Then a long, low hum, powerful, electrical, and lightning glistening off the slick walls. *The third rail. The water*. She could hear moans and screams. Death by electrocution. But it was coming down their way too.

She picked up the little girl, took Del's hand, and ran, lightning bouncing off the wet, tracking the surface. They managed to keep a step ahead, the water even growing more shallow, until the hum stopped, and the sewer went pitch black.

They kept running, by flashlight now, descending through the stink, past smaller tunnels feeding in, always taking the fork to the bigger opening, leading down. The water was brown, green, and milky. And the concrete ceiling got lower and turned to rough-hewn timber. A buried river, built over by a growing city, unmindful of its past.

Then brick and concrete and a flash through another grating. The street above. Light—sunrise, and
men looking, searching, but not knowing their prey was
just underfoot.

There was a circle of white in the distance. The end
of the tunnel, unexpected.

26

THE WATER FELL OUT the opening into the mouth of the Bronx River. They were in a runoff tunnel, not deep enough.

"We have to find the main sewer line, under the bay," she told him.

She knew there'd be an airshaft. There always was in a sewer line to release the gases, stop an explosion. All that decomposing bio matter. So she followed her nose back up the tunnel, to where the smell concentrated, thick with methane, about 100 feet in. Looking through the muck, she couldn't find the source, the walls caked with slime. The sounds of people came from deeper inside the tunnel, from where they had just come.

They could make a beeline for the end, go into the river. Jess looked over, down to the opening. The light was harsh now, the sun shining directly in. And now, there was the silhouette of a man. Closing in on both ends, they had them trapped. But the light from the sun, caught a piece of metal halfway up the wall, poking out, bent, from the algae.

She pushed her fingers in. The airshaft. She found it. Another grating. This one, light mesh, pulled free with a quick yank.

She went up and in first. The girl followed then Del, squeezing through more easily this time with the algae as lubricant. It was a tight space, horizontal, and it stunk like a garbage dump. The reinforced concrete was broken in spots, revealing iron rods, rusting into the cement. Jess crawled through as fast as she could, looking back every few moments to make sure the other two were behind her.

With her eyes pointing the other way, her hand dropped onto empty space. She almost fell headlong through the hole. Looking down in with the flashlight, she saw the turgid waters of a large sewer. She threw back her hand, signaling to Del. It was quiet for a moment, and she could hear the men in the runoff tunnel behind them. She cut the light, jockeyed her body around, and jumped feet first into the lower sewer.

The waters almost swept her away, but she caught herself on a metal ladder built into the side wall. She pointed to it with the light, guiding the little girl down, and then Del.

They ran through the water, a putrid rapids, descending further. The water came up, knee-high, waist-high, then up to her chest, then her neck. Del held the little girl up, and Jess prayed the water wouldn't get any deeper. Her head brushed the ceiling. Another few inches, and they'd be underwater.

She figured, hoped, they were under Eastchester Bay now, in the main sewer line, buried under the mud. But the water kept getting higher until it hit the ceiling. And now, noise behind them—men dropping down, back in the distance, splashing, swishing, men in pursuit.

"I'll take the girl," Del whispered in her ear, in the darkness.

Even then, she wanted to tell him that she loved him but couldn't.

She went under, down in the muck, swimming for thirty, forty, fifty seconds, faster, feeling the ceiling, still no air. She felt Del's hand against her ankle, taking her mind off her lungs, about to explode, for a split second. Her own hand brushed the ceiling again, and she felt it, a bow, a curve, convex, in the surface. They were coming up off the bottom, the low point. If they could just make it a little further, there'd be air again.

She pushed and swam until she felt the cold on her fingers. A little further, and her hand was free too. Then her face, and cold gasps of air. Del . . . the little girl . . . . She waited. But there was still no Del, no Jenny. Terror in her heart, she thought to go back under, but they had to come back up. Ten seconds seemed like ten minutes, and she swallowed a mouthful of air to go back. But the surface broke before she had a chance.

Her little girl was gasping, choking, her tiny lungs straining for precious oxygen. No time to worry. She was okay. They moved ahead, the water subsiding, until they were able to run again, now only shin-deep, coming off the bottom. It had to be the bay, Jess thought, almost willing it to be so.

They ran through the sewer, up a slight grade, until the water barely covered their shoes, until they came to a fork. Del looked at her, silent, and again, the moment echoed the sounds of feet in water, behind them, not far. She didn't know which way to go, left or right, taking only a second to ponder it. *The mainland to the left, the island to the right*, she thought. It was as good a guess as any.

The grade was steeper, and the sounds pursuing them got closer. Then, a sliver of daylight—a storm drain. And another iron ladder leading up a cement tube a few feet away. A manhole cover.

Del went up first, pushing it off. Daylight came down on her, shining off the little girl's blond hair. Jess pushed her up then popped her own head out, pulling herself up after. *City Island. King Avenue.*

A half mile off, over on the mainland, a horde of them were in a sprint, coming their way.

"The bridge," she told Del, running down the street, towards the crossing to High Island. She resisted the urge to look over to where her house had been or the other way, to the approaching mass. The bridge was there, as it had always been, just off the junction with Terrace Street.

A chain linked gate, locked, and a sign marked "No Entry" greeted them. A nest of barbed wire on top stopped her cold. But Del jumped up and pushed it aside, even as it cut him. He held a small hole open, and Jess pushed Jenny through, slipping by after. A barb cut her side, but she was over.

The bridge was wooden but solid, with chain link fencing at both sides. It was wide enough for a car, and the three of them ran side-by-side, Jess practically dragging the little girl, her feet struggling to keep up.

The horde was only a few minutes behind when Jess's foot hit the opposite shore. Looking up, she could see the red and white tower, still intact. Below, on the ground, a small weather-beaten mobile home—the caretaker's house. It was laid out in two sections. The control room and broadcast booth would be inside the smaller one, no bigger than a shack.

She tore through a gate that warned "WFAN 660 AM. No Trespassing," and ran to the door. Locked. Del pushed her out of the way and kicked it in. Jess thought the whole place would collapse under the blow.

Inside, she found the control room. She knew she didn't have long. She hadn't been in a broadcast booth since she was at Poly, but it wasn't complicated. The power was already on, a broadcast going out. She cut it off and set the frequency she needed—1257 Megahertz. She could hear them coming over the bridge, hitting the island, as she went to hit the switch. Then the power went dead.

"They cut the power!" she screamed, looking at him and her little girl.

They were resolved, calm, and brave, and it made her proud, but she wasn't ready to give up. Not yet.

"Auxiliary power," she said, looking around, her eye catching the fuse box and a lever next to it.

They were at the house now, coming in. She pulled the handle.

"Hit the broadcast switch!" she yelled at Del.

He reached over and hit the button. The red light went on. *Live.* The side of his shirt was soaked with blood, and the tear from the barbed wire revealed a hole in the skin underneath. She realized he'd been shot back in the runoff tunnel when he was stuck. Blood oozed when his muscles tightened, and she noticed him struggling. One of them had him in his grip.

She pulled him off, then another one came. This one never made it, collapsing in the doorway. And then another one. She stepped outside, watching them drop into the grass, on the path, the bridge, and even into the water. She knew then that it had worked. In a few minutes, they'd all be dead.

By the time she went back to her little girl, it was too late. Her face was green, and she looked at Jess one last time, before her eyes rolled back into her head. Jess stumbled through the door, reaching her a step ahead of Del.

"What's wrong?" he asked.

Jess didn't know, couldn't understand. She opened her lips to give her mouth-to-mouth. *That'll save her.* Then she saw the girl's gums. Clean. The thin line of lead was gone, finally flushed completely out of her system.

"Lead! It interferes with iron metabolism," she said in an epiphany.

She wasn't immune like they were, like they had figured. The lead had just masked the symptoms, stopped the prions from infecting her. Until now. Jess had figured it out, but it was too late, and she knew it.

"I have to stop the broadcast, turn it off!"

"No, Jess!" Del yelled, stopping her.

She fell back against the wall and coddled the little girl's head.

Tears streamed down Jess's face as she held her. "I'm sorry. I'm so, so sorry," and she uttered the words she had longed to hear, "I love you . . . I love you . . ."

About the Author

The author of seven books, Seth Edgarde holds advanced degrees in Applied Mathematics and Computer Science from Brown University as well as a degree in Physics from the University of Chicago. *Lumina* is his first science fiction novel.

To see our other great titles,
visit us at:

BLACKBIRD BOOKS
www.bbirdbooks.com